JACKIE BRAUN

Mr. Right There All Along

The Fun Factor

Harlequin®

TORONTO NEW YORK LONDON
AMSTERDAM PARIS SYDNEY HAMBURG
STOCKHOLM ATHENS TOKYO MILAN MADRID
PRAGUE WARSAW BUDAPEST AUCKLAND

Recycling programs
for this product may
not exist in your area.

ISBN-13: 978-0-373-17748-6

MR. RIGHT THERE ALL ALONG

First North American Publication 2011

Copyright © 2011 by Jackie Braun Fridline

www.Harlequin.com

Printed in U.S.A.

Jackie Braun is a three-time RITA® Award finalist, a four-time National Readers' Choice Awards finalist and the winner of a Rising Star Award for traditional romantic fiction. She can be reached through her website at www.jackiebraun.com.

"I remember the first time I saw the man who would become my husband. I thought he was gorgeous and had a nice butt. What I didn't know then was that he also had a terrific sense of humor and a contagious laugh. Nor did I know that he would eventually become my dearest friend."— Jackie Braun

For my husband, Mark.
We've had lots of reasons to cry.
We've chosen to laugh instead.
That—and you—have made all
the difference in my life. I love you.

CHAPTER ONE

High School History 101

WHEN SHE SPIED the invitation amid the pile of bills and junk mail, Chloe McDaniels's lips pulled back in a sneer. She'd been expecting it, but that didn't make her reaction any less visceral.

Tillman High School's Class of 2001 was set to celebrate its ten-year reunion.

Chloe did not have fond memories of her New Jersey high school. In fact, she'd spent her four years at Tillman ducking into bathroom stalls and janitors' broom closets to avoid the unholy trinity of Natasha Bradford, Faith Ellerman and Tamara Kingsley.

She'd known the girls since grade school. They'd never been friends, but neither had they been enemies... until the start of their freshman year when, for reasons that had never been terribly clear to Chloe, she'd become their favorite target.

Literally.

Somehow on that first, already awkward day of high school, they managed to attach a "Kick Me" sign to the back of her shirt just before the start of first period. It was the last time Chloe ever accepted a friendly back slap without taking a gander over her shoulder afterward. As cruel pranks went, it wasn't terribly original, but it was effective. She'd taken enough sneakers to the seat of her favorite jeans to feel like a soccer ball.

Then, between third period and lunch, Simon Ford had happened along.

"You might not want to wear this," he'd said simply, removing the sign and handing it to Chloe. That was his way. Understated.

Good old Simon. He always had her back. Or backside, as the case had been. They'd been friends since his family had moved into her family's apartment building at the start of third grade and their friendship continued to this day. Thinking of him now, Chloe picked up the phone before realizing the time. It was well after five on a Friday. He was probably out with his girlfriend.

Chloe realized she was sneering again. Well, it couldn't be helped. She didn't like Sara. The long-limbed and lithe blonde was too...too...perfect.

She glanced down at the invitation. Perfect Sara would never find herself in this position. Perfect Sara would have been the homecoming queen and the prom queen and the every other kind of queen at her high school. Unlike Chloe, whose only class recognition had come in the form of "curliest hair" and "most freckles."

Yeah, that was what a girl wanted to be remembered for, all right.

Her gut told her to ball up the invitation in a wad, spit

on it and, with expletives she knew in four languages, send it whizzing into the trash can. Her heart was a different matter. It was telling her to reach for a spoon and the pint of mint chocolate chip ice cream in her freezer.

Diet in mind, she went with her gut.

Sort of.

She lavished the invitation with every foreign epithet she could think of before heaving it in the trash. But, while she bypassed the ice cream, she booted up her computer and downloaded a recipe from her favorite cable cooking show, *Susie Kay's Comfort Foods*. If it was all but guaranteed to clog the arteries and contribute to heart disease, Susie Kay made it.

Tonight's dinner selection was a case in point. Macaroni and cheese with not one, but four kinds of cheese and enough butter and calories that Chloe swore her clothes fit tighter just reading the ingredients. Not good considering she was already wearing her fat pants.

Actually, the pants were elastic-waist exercise gear that she didn't exercise in but instead reserved for days when she felt particularly bloated. Today was just such a day. Strap a few cables to her and she would be right at home gliding down Sixth Avenue like one of those huge helium balloons in the annual Thanksgiving Day parade. Even so, that didn't keep her from making the mac and cheese and eating half of the six servings.

The wine she poured for herself was an afterthought. She'd been saving the pricey bottle of cabernet sauvignon for a special occasion. This definitely was not it, but three glasses later, she didn't care.

Chloe set the wine aside and went to her stereo. Music. That's what she needed now. Something with a wicked beat and a lot of bass. Something she could dance to with reckless abandon and maybe work off a few extra calories in the process. She chose…Céline Dion.

As one weepy ballad after another filled Chloe's Lower East Side studio apartment, her willpower wilted like the water-deprived basil plant on her kitchen windowsill. Again muttering foreign curses, this time aimed at herself, she fished the crumpled invitation out of the trash. When the telephone rang, she was still sitting on the kitchen floor smoothing out the wrinkles.

It was Simon.

"Hey, Chloe. What are you doing?"

Anyone else—her older and über-chic sister, Frannie, for instance—and Chloe would have felt compelled to come up with some elaborate reason why she could be found home alone on the official start of the weekend.

Since it was Simon, she confessed, "Drinking wine, wearing Lycra and listening to the soundtrack from *Titanic*."

"No ice cream?"

How well he knew her. Despite her best intentions, the mint chocolate chip was next on her list. "Not yet."

"Want some company?" he asked.

Did she ever. She and Simon always had a good time together, whether it involved going out or just hanging out. Still, his question surprised her. Wasn't he supposed to be with his girlfriend tonight? She liked thinking he'd throw over Perfect Sara to be with Comfortable Chloe. Liked it so much that she immediately felt guilty. She was a terrible friend. To make up for it, she would share her ice cream and what was left of the wine.

"When can I expect you?"

"Right now. I'm standing on the other side of your apartment door."

If he were a boyfriend—not that Chloe had had one of *those* in several months—this news would have sent her into a panic. Her apartment was a mess. For that matter, so was she. Her red hair was a riot of curls thanks to the day's high humidity. And what little makeup she'd applied that morning was long gone. But this was Simon. *Simon,* she reminded herself, after a glance down at her unflattering attire had her wanting to flee to her bedroom and change.

It was sad to admit, but he'd seen her looking worse. Much worse. Such as when she came down with the chicken pox in the sixth grade or the time in high school when she'd succumbed to salmonella after her cousin Ellen's bridal shower. Aunt Myrtle made the chicken salad, which was why, henceforth, the woman was only allowed to bring paper products or plastic cutlery to family gatherings. The coup de grâce, of course, was last December. Three days shy of Christmas, the guy Chloe had been dating for the previous six months dumped her.

Via text message.

And she'd already bought him a gift, a Rolex watch, which she couldn't return since the street vendor who'd sold her the incredibly authentic-looking knockoff had moved to a new location.

So, now, she flung open the door, feeling only mildly embarrassed by what her hair was doing, by the mac-and-cheese stains on her shirt or the fact that her lips had probably turned a slightly clownish shade of purple from the wine she'd enjoyed.

"Hey, Simon."

As usual, his smile made her feel as if seeing her was the highlight of his day.

"Hey, gorgeous." He kissed her cheek as he always did before waving a slim, square box beneath her nose. "I've got pizza. Thin crust with extra cheese from that new Italian place just shy of Fourteenth."

Any other time, the aroma of pepperoni and melted mozzarella would have had her salivating. Right now, it reminded her of how full she felt. "Thanks, but I just finishing eating."

His gaze took in the stained shirt. The sides of his mouth lifted. "So I see. What was on today's menu and why?"

Yes, he knew her way too well.

"Mac and cheese."

"Ah." He nodded sagely. "Comfort food."

She touched an index finger to the tip of her nose. "You got it in one."

He smiled in return. Simon had a great smile. She'd always thought so. With perfectly proportioned lips in a face that wasn't drop-dead gorgeous but handsome and pleasingly male. Over the years, his cheeks had gotten leaner and more sculpted-looking, but his ready smile kept him from ever looking hard.

"How much did you eat?" he asked.

"Too much."

"Save me any?" He glanced in the direction of the stove.

"Enough." She tapped the box he held. "What about your pizza?"

He shrugged. "You know pizza. It's even better cold." Then, with the pad of his thumb, he pressed down on her lower lip. She ignored the sensation his touch sent coursing up her spine. "And what about the wine? Did you save me any of that?"

Chloe laughed. How did other women manage to drink a few glasses of cab and not wind up with stained lips? For that matter, how did other women manage to eat a meal's worth of carbs and not have to do deep knee bends so they could breathe in their jeans?

"There's almost half a bottle," she told him.

"Pour me a glass and tell me about your day."

He set the pizza box on the kitchen counter and shrugged out of his trench coat. He was wearing his usual business attire—crisp white shirt and tailored suit with a perfectly folded handkerchief peeking from its breast pocket. The matching silk tie, however, was pulled askew. It struck Chloe then. "Did you just come from work?"

It was nearly eight o'clock.

"The merger with that other software company I mentioned is eating up a lot of my spare time." He dropped heavily into one of the kitchen chairs.

How had she missed how tired he looked? She wanted to go to him, wrap him in her arms. Friends hugged. But she held back. More and more lately, she found herself doing that. She blamed Perfect Sara and the bevy of beauties that had come before her.

"Sorry to hear that." She switched on the stove to reheat the mac and cheese, and poured him a glass of wine. After handing it to him, she stood behind his chair and began kneading the knotted muscles in his neck and shoulders.

His moan of pleasure nearly made her stop. Instead, she kept at it and asked, "So, how does Sara feel about the long hours you're keeping?"

"Not happy," he admitted. His tone was rueful when he said, "We were supposed to go to a Broadway show tonight."

"You stood her up?" That wasn't like him. Simon was the kindest, most considerate man Chloe knew... even if he had really lousy taste in women.

"Ouch!"

Apparently, she'd massaged a little too vigorously.

"Sorry."

"Actually, when I called to tell her I was running late and we'd have to skip dinner beforehand, she told me to go... Never mind." He shook his head. "It doesn't matter. The relationship wasn't heading anywhere anyway."

Jubilation.

Before Chloe could help it, the feeling bubbled up inside her with all of the effervescence of champagne. Maybe this day didn't totally stink after all.

However, because she knew a friend wasn't supposed to feel happy upon hearing such news, she kept her expression sympathetic when she slid into the chair opposite his.

"Ooh. Dumped. Sorry."

"It was mutual," he muttered, reaching for his wine. "Sara just said it first."

"Okaaaay."

"My heart's not broken, Chloe. Hell, it's not even dented or mildly scratched." He sipped his wine and sighed heavily before squinting at her. "That's not right, is it? I should feel…a little sad, shouldn't I?"

"You don't?"

Jubilation made another appearance, but she carefully tucked it behind a bland expression.

"Not one bit." He studied his wine a moment before his gaze lifted to hers. "I guess we weren't suited."

No kidding. It had taken him nearly a year to figure that out? Chloe had concluded as much within mere minutes of meeting Sara for the first time.

"But that's neither here nor there," Simon was saying. He rallied with a smile. "We were going to talk about your day."

Her day. *Ick!*

Chloe rose and went to the stove to plate his dinner. She opened the fridge and got out a sprig of fresh parsley to add to the mac and cheese before bringing it to the table. Simon's eyebrows rose.

"Appearances are everything," she said, setting the plate before him with a flourish.

He picked up his fork and pointed the tines in her direction. "That's exactly your problem, Chloe."

It was an old observation. Under normal circumstances, it wouldn't have bothered her. Tonight, however, she snapped in exasperation, "Do you want to analyze me or do you want me to tell you about my day?"

"Actually, I want you to tell me about *that*." Again, he used the tines of his fork to point, this time toward the class reunion invitation that, somewhere between belting out "My Heart Will Go On" and hearing about Simon's newly single status, Chloe had forgotten all about.

She shrugged, striving for nonchalance. "It seems our ten-year reunion is right around the corner."

"I know. My invitation arrived in the mail last week."

"Last week? Are you kidding? We live in the same city, practically in the same zip code. I bet the unholy trio had something to do with that," she alleged.

So much for nonchalance.

"Chloe, really. It's been ten years." Simon said it in that patient way of his that usually served to talk her down from whatever ledge she was on.

Not on this day. Nope. She was poised to jump, ushered to the edge of reason by the wine and some very unhappy memories.

"Seems like yesterday to me," she muttered.

Damn the cabernet for her loose lips. Even so, she reached for her glass now and took a liberal sip while she waited for Simon's well-reasoned rebuttal.

It didn't come.

"So, are you going?" he asked.

"Am I going?" she repeated incredulously. She returned her wineglass to the table with a smart click. "You're kidding, right?" The question was rhetorical and they both knew it, so she plowed ahead. "You couldn't pay me enough to make so much as a token appearance at that thing. I'd rather give up ice cream for…for… *forever* than to step foot in the…" She craned her neck to read the invitation. The outrage whooshed out of her and she snorted. "The Tillman High gymnasium? Gee, that's classy. They couldn't spring for a banquet hall or something?"

"I don't know. I rather like the idea of seeing the old school again, even if I never spent much time in the gym."

Simon laughed then. He'd been a geek, not a jock. Chess club, computer club, debate team—those sorts of interests had been his thing. And Chloe's, too. His geek status had never bothered him as much as hers had bothered her.

Her gaze narrowed. "Wait a minute. Do you mean you're going to the reunion?"

Simon regarded her over his wineglass. Actually, he hadn't planned to attend until just that moment. Chloe needed to go. He'd never met anyone so haunted by high school. The invitation's crumpled appearance was a testament to that, as was her mac-and-cheese binge and wine indulgence.

She'd grown into a lovely, bright, funny and creative young woman. But then, he'd always found her lovely and funny, bright and creative. She, however, still entertained a ridiculously warped view of herself. It was time she exorcised her demons. To do that, she had to face the past. But he couldn't, wouldn't, send her into the lion's den alone.

"Sure. Why wouldn't I?" he asked.

"Did we or did we not attend the same high school?" Purple-hued lips turned down in a frown. He had to be crazy, but he still found those lips incredibly sexy.

And that was his problem. And the reason why women like Sara never lasted for very long. They simply couldn't measure up to Chloe.

"Those days are over," he told her, taking her hand in one of his. "Those girls have nothing on you, Chloe. They never did."

"They made my life hell!"

"They were cruel," he agreed in a tone more moderated than hers. "But they can't make your life hell now, unless you let them. Go back, face them and show them how far you've come since high school. You've got a lot to be proud of."

"Yeah, right." She pulled her hand free. "I'm twenty-eight years old, single, working part-time and living with an antisocial cat."

Simon waved hand. "All cats are antisocial. I told

you to get a dog if you wanted companionship from a pet."

She crossed her arms over her chest. "Must you lecture me now?"

"It seems so." He waited a beat before asking, "Are we going together? Or are you bringing a date?"

"A date." She frowned, apparently realizing what she'd said. Her hands fell to her sides. "How do you do that?"

"What?"

"Talk me into doing something that I absolutely don't want to do?"

"Years of practice," he replied.

"Okay. Since *you* think I need to do this, I will."

"Thanks."

"But only because I know you'll hold it over my head forever if I don't." She ended on a long-suffering sigh.

They both knew it was a cover and that she was grateful for the push.

"You'll thank me someday," he said.

"Or I'll blame you indefinitely for the years of therapy to follow."

"I'll take my chances." He shrugged and started in again on the mac and cheese. It was good, nearly as mouthwatering as Chloe's pout.

She was quiet while he finished off the last of the pasta, which was never a good sign. It meant she was thinking. More accurately, it meant she was plotting.

Sure enough, just as he blotted his mouth with a napkin, she said, "You don't mind if I go with someone else, do you? We can still sit together." Her expression brightened. "You can bring someone, too. We can double-date. That will be fun."

Simon ignored the twinge in his chest. He always felt it when Chloe talked about other men. In fact, one of the things Sara had flung in his face that evening during their breakup was what she termed his "unhealthy attachment to *that woman.*"

Sara wasn't the first girlfriend to mention it. Nor, he suspected, would she be the last. He *was* attached to Chloe. How could he not be? They'd been close friends since before puberty and had seen one another through the good, the bad and the ugly of adolescence. They'd also been there for one another through high school and college and, now, the better part of their twenties. She was the only constant in his life.

"Well?" Chloe was frowning, and obviously waiting for his reply.

"Why would I mind?" Even to his ears, the words came out sounding hollow and defensive. He cleared his throat and shifted the conversation in a new direction. "I didn't know you were seeing someone."

"I'm not. But I plan to come up with the best-looking, most successful guy I can find, even if I have to pay him to attend with me."

Oh, yeah. Those wheels had been turning, all right.

"Chloe, really—"

She cut him off. "Yes, *really.* I want Natasha, Faith and Tamara to take one look at the hunk I'm with and drool an Olympic-size swimming pool."

"That'll show 'em," he drawled.

She nodded, oblivious to his sarcasm.

"Where do you plan to meet this Adonis?" God, please, tell him that she wasn't going to say the internet. He'd talked her out of cyberspace dating twice already.

Her smile was overly bright despite the fact that her teeth were tinted the same shade of purple as her lips. He knew he was in trouble even before she said, "I remember seeing a really attractive guy at your office the last time I stopped in to see you. Trevor something. I think you mentioned that he was a lawyer helping you with some of the details on your merger."

Uh-uh. No way was Simon going to set her up with Trevor, or, as the ladies at his company had dubbed him, "Mr. Hottie." He would be only too glad to have the merger behind him so he could cut the guy loose. Productivity among the women at Ford Technology Solutions came to a standstill whenever Trevor was around.

"No."

"Please." She clasped her hands in front of her. "Pretty please?"

Her smile, purple-tinted or not, was nearly Simon's undoing. God knew, as it was, he would do anything short of murder for the woman, and even that was negotiable. But, he managed to remain firm. "I'm sorry, Chloe, but no."

"All right." She nodded. "I understand. I mean, it's not as if I've *ever* done *you* a huge favor or anything."

It was all he could do to suppress a groan, because the list was long and, no doubt, Chloe planned to launch into it at any moment. Simon sighed and capitulated with the grace of a man being pushed to his death.

"Fine. All right."

"Thank you!"

"I make no promises."

"I know. I don't expect promises."

Which was exactly why Simon, to his everlasting regret, meant it when he said, "I'll see what I can do."

CHAPTER TWO

Cramming for Finals

THE FIRST THING Chloe did when she woke the next morning—after trying to rub off the worst of the wine stains from her lips—was to boot up her computer and make a list of all the things she needed to do before the reunion.

Six weeks.

That's all she had. It wasn't a lot of time…and she had a lot to do. Well, no problem. She was the queen of self-improvement. She'd had enough practice at it—she had an entire library of books in her apartment on the subject. More might be in order, she decided, thinking of a show she'd seen earlier in the week.

She prioritized her needs as she created the list.

First and foremost, she would whip herself into the best physical shape possible. Since this had been a regular New Year's resolution since her late teen years, she was familiar with the format. But rather than mere diet and exercise, the reunion timeframe called for a boot-camp mentality.

If she had to forgo ice cream, so be it. The same for her favorite bagels, pasta, comfort food and…food in general. She'd work out five—no, *seven*—days a week. And really work out. Not just don the outfits and sit in a smoothie bar, pretending to have just come from aerobics class. She'd even give in and accompany Simon on his morning runs in Central Park. He was always after her to join him.

Running. Hmm.

She tapped her bottom lip thoughtfully as she gazed at the computer screen. In parentheses next to the bit on exercise, she wrote: *Shape wear.*

She wasn't above a little cheating, as proved by the padded push-up bras she wore on a regular basis. As her mother was fond of saying, "What God has forgotten can be fixed up with cotton." Or synthetic filling, as the case may be. So why not reduce the appearance of a muffin top and jiggly bottom with a discreet foundation garment?

After all, realistically speaking, there was only so much one could do in six weeks. Chloe leaned back in the chair and folded her arms over her middle. She could feel the subtle roll just above the elastic waistband of her pajama bottoms. She straightened.

Shape wear, definitely.

Besides, celebrities and beauty-pageant contestants did it all the time. Heck, they did more than that to acquire their perky breasts and sag-free butts, so that everyone sighed with envy as they watched them strut the stage in Atlantic City or glide up the red carpet on premier night.

Which reminded Chloe. She needed a killer outfit to show off the killer curves she was planning to acquire through either sweat or spandex.

She typed, *Little black dress, emphasis on little.*

Smiling, she pictured it. Something sleek and clinging...okay, and with subtle ruching around the waist to distract from any flaws that remained despite the shape wear. Her legs, from mid-thigh down, would be the star of the show, which made sense since they remained her best attribute. Even when she gained weight, the extra pounds tended to collect at her hips and middle rather than on her thighs. And she had nice calves. They were shapely without looking like they belonged on a bicycle messenger. Put her in a pair of high heels and she could be a pinup...well, from mid-thigh down.

Heels. *Ooh.* She would have to practice walking in them. She'd never been very steady on anything higher than a couple of inches.

Stilettos, she typed.

That was what she had in mind to go with the sexy, stingy bit of black fabric that was going to pass for her dress.

Was black the best color for her? She studied her arms. Her skin was pale. Like most redheads, she had a tendency to freckle, which was why she stayed out of the sun whenever possible. Black brought out her most, well, *ghostly* hue. But if not black, then what?

Given her hair color, she generally steered clear of

reds and oranges. Pink was out, too. She didn't care for purple. It reminded her too much of eggplant, and she hated that vegetable on principle. She'd barfed up an entire plate-worth of eggplant parmesan in the cafeteria her freshman year, earning her the unfortunate nickname Yack-Attack.

Green would do in a pinch, though paired with her hair it made her feel a little too much like a pumpkin. As for blue...uh-uh.

She hated blue.

Any and all shades, but especially baby blue for reasons far more emotional than aesthetic. She'd worn a formal dress that color to her senior prom. Her mother had talked her into it, claiming it flattered her figure, when in fact the full skirt made it appear she was trying to smuggle someone into the dance.

She could still recall how humiliated she'd felt when Natasha and company had cornered her on the dance floor and pulled up her skirt to see if she was alone.

She'd been alone and wearing a pair of briefs the likes of which would have been right at home on her Nana.

Chloe shuddered now. Black it was. With thong panties. Under shape wear.

She'd compensate for her pale complexion with a salon-bought tan. Not the sort that involved lying on a bed under UV rays. That would only bring out her freckles, and Chloe hated her freckles, even if Simon had once commented that he found them adorable. She didn't believe him. After all, none of the women he'd ever dated had freckles. If he liked them as much as he claimed, the women in his life should have resembled leopards.

Chloe decided to go with a spray-on tan. Her sister had gotten such a treatment before her wedding the year before. Of course, Frannie was a brunette and her skin wasn't nearly as pale as Chloe's, but Frannie had come away with a nice, healthy glow. She was always after Chloe to try it.

The phone rang as she shot her sister an email asking for the name of her salon.

"Hello?"

"Good morning," Simon replied. "I'm going for coffee at the Filigree Café. Want to meet me there? I'll spring for the bagels."

The Filigree served some of the best coffee and homemade baked goods in Lower Manhattan. She and Simon met there on weekend mornings when neither of them had other plans. That was often the case for Chloe. Not so much lately for Simon, but then his dating status had changed.

Once again, she ignored jubilation, as well as the way her mouth watered at the mere thought of a toasted onion bagel with herbed cream cheese.

"Sorry. No bagels for me. I'm on a diet," she informed him.

"Since when?"

"Since when not?" she replied. "I'm always on a diet." Which, sadly enough, was all too true.

A wise man, Simon didn't point out that this had

never stopped her from joining him for a bagel in the past. Instead, he asked, "Is this about the reunion?"

"No."

They both knew she was lying.

"Come on, Chloe. Join me. What's the fun in eating alone?"

"Simon…"

"We'll go for a walk afterward," he promised. "A long, brisk one. It's a great morning for it. No humidity and the temperatures aren't supposed to reach into the eighties until this afternoon."

She pulled at her curly hair, and relented. "Okay. But I'm not having a bagel."

"Agreed. And I won't let you have so much as a bite of mine."

"You're humoring me," she accused.

"I'm dead serious. Meet you there in half an hour?"

The old Chloe would have said yes. The brand-new and improved Chloe knew that half an hour would barely give her enough time to brush her teeth and hair and throw on whatever clean clothes she could find hiding amid the heaps of laundry on her bedroom floor.

"Make it an hour. I'm not even dressed or anything."

"An hour?" Simon sounded surprised and no wonder given their long history as friends. "You *really* need an hour to get dressed?"

"I'm turning over a new leaf. I want to actually wear makeup and look presentable when I appear in public. Even if it's just with you," she replied drily.

"Okay, an hour." Rather than sounding irritated, he almost sounded intrigued. "I'll get our usual corner table. See you then."

Simon was on his third cup of coffee when Chloe finally arrived at the cafe. It was hard to be angry with her given the way she looked. She didn't primp often, but when she did… Wow! He sucked in a breath and reached for his cup, failing in his determination not to admire the way her jeans hugged her hips or the way the vee of her shirt offered the slightest hint of cleavage.

She thought she needed to lose weight. When she dressed like this, he thought he'd lose his mind.

She was wearing makeup, not a lot, but enough to enhance her long lashes and bring out the cool green in her eyes. And her hair. No quick and easy ponytail intended to disguise its lovely and natural waves. No. She'd left it down in a riot of curls that framed her face and fell past her shoulders.

It was wrong of him, Simon knew, but he almost wished she'd shown up in baggy sweats and a T-shirt, no makeup and that dreadful, all-purpose ponytail. Then, at least, he wouldn't feel so damned interested and, well, needy.

He chanced a glance around and regretted it. Sure enough, several of the other male patrons were checking her out. He didn't like their interested expressions. Not one damn bit. Before he could stop himself, he pushed to his feet. The legs of his chair scraped noisily over the tiled floor. They seemed to scream, "Back off! She's mine."

The attention was on him now. All of the attention, including Chloe's. Her face lit up when she spied him and a pair of full lips pulled into a smile that was sexy without trying to be. How was it possible, he wondered for the millionth time, that a woman as naturally lovely as she was had self-esteem issues?

He shot a smug look at each of the guys who'd been ogling her, and took his time kissing her cheek when she reached the table.

"Sorry I'm late," she said as she slid onto the chair opposite his.

Simon shrugged. "It was worth the wait. Look at you. The hair, the makeup, the cleav...clean clothes," he amended hastily, forcing his gaze back up to her face.

She grinned. "So, you like?"

"Of course I do. So do half the guys in here, judging from the way they were watching you."

"Yeah?" Her face brightened and she glanced around. "Which ones?"

He unclenched his teeth and forced out a laugh. "Forget it. I'm not going to stroke your ego any more than I already have."

"Spoilsport," she replied.

Her expression said she didn't believe him. He considered relenting. He should throw her a bone—or a whole roomful of them. But their waitress arrived then. She was a heavyset woman named Helga with a thick accent of Eastern European origin. The woman had been waiting on them for half a decade. Even so, she eyed Chloe curiously before asking, "Your usual today?"

Chloe's usual was a double mocha latte and toasted onion bagel slathered with enough melted butter and cream cheese that it should have come with an American Heart Association warning.

"Not today. I'll have coffee, black. Make it decaf."

"And to eat?"

"Nothing."

Helga's bushy eyebrows shot up at that. "You no want something to eat?"

"No. Nothing."

"You feel okay?"

"Fine. I'm on a diet," she confessed.

"Chloe's always on a diet," Simon inserted.

Helga made a rude sound. "Girls nowadays, they all want to be so skinny. Too skinny, I think. A stiff breeze, they blow over." She motioned with her notepad, before turning to Simon. "So, you think she need to lose weight?"

"No. Not a pound." She was perfect in his book. Always had been.

"See." Helga nodded vigorously. To Chloe, she said, "I bring you onion bagel just how you like."

Chloe's expression turned panicked, but before she could refuse, Simon said casually, "You don't have to eat all of it. Or any of it, Chloe. Consider it a test of your willpower."

"Fine." She straightened in her seat and squared her shoulders, making the display of her cleavage even harder for Simon to ignore. It was like a magnet, drawing his gaze.

"What will you have?" Helga asked.

Because he knew what he really wanted was off-limits, he wrapped both hands around his cup of coffee and forced his gaze to the stocky waitress. "Two slices of whole wheat toast and a fruit cup."

Helga pursed her lips in distaste as she jotted down his order. "Fruit cup," she muttered as she walked away. "Is whole world on diet?"

"I think we've ruined her day," Chloe said.

"We'll leave a big tip," Simon replied.

They always did, regardless of the amount they spent. The way Simon saw it, she deserved the tip. He and Chloe took up one of Helga's prime tables for at least a couple of hours on a Saturday without running up a sizable tab.

Chloe fussed with her hair, pulling it back behind her head. No doubt if she had a rubber band at her disposal, it would wind up in a ponytail.

"I like your hair down," he said.

On a sigh, she let it drop. "It's not even humid out and my hair is already going nuts. You wouldn't know I'd used this expensive new antifrizz stuff. I want my money back."

"I don't know. I think it looks nice. I like it when you leave it curly."

"I don't mind curly, but it's heading toward steel wool. For the reunion, I'm thinking of having it professionally straightened."

Don't! He wanted to shout. But he doubted she would follow his advice. So, instead he lifted his shoulders. "Whatever you think best."

Helga was back with Chloe's coffee and refilled Simon's cup.

"I'm considering dying it a different color, too." She smiled at their waitress. "What do you think? Should I attempt blond?"

Helga issued that rude sound again. Before stalking away, she said, "Keep what God gave you."

To Simon, Chloe said, "I think God could have been a little more generous in certain areas and, well, spread the wealth in others, if you know what I mean."

"You wouldn't look good as a blonde."

She frowned. "I thought you liked blondes? The last three women you dated all looked like they just stepped out of the California sun."

True enough, he realized, although it hadn't been intentional. They'd been available and interested and, well, since he'd been available... He didn't like how that made it seem, though he'd never pretended to have deep feelings for any of them. Nor had he made any promises.

He wasn't his father...a man who made promises, vows even, with the ease of a politician, only to break them, as wives one through five could attest.

"Simon?" Chloe was staring at him.

He pulled himself back to the present. "Your coloring is all wrong for blond hair. You're too fair."

"That can be changed, too."

He didn't like the glint in her eye. "Please tell me you're not thinking about tanning again. Remember what happened before senior pictures."

She shuddered, making him sorry to have brought it up. She'd gotten the bright idea to lie under the heat lamp her grandmother kept to warm new litters of Persian kittens, and had wound up burned to the point of blistering on her cheeks and the bridge of her nose.

"Not tanning per se," she murmured, but before he could question her further, she asked, "Will you be going for your usual run tomorrow morning?"

He frowned at the change in subject. "Why?"

"I was thinking of joining you."

He couldn't help it. His brows shot up. "Are you going to run?"

She wrinkled her nose, a sign she was insulted. "You don't need to look so shocked. Haven't you pestered me since Nana's heart attack to do more cardio conditioning?"

He had indeed, worried that Chloe's addiction to comfort food might take her down the same hardened-arteries path as her seventy-four-year-old grandmother. But he knew Chloe's sudden decision to listen had less to do with his persuasive abilities than their upcoming class reunion. He almost called her on it. But the truth was, he liked the idea of having company during the runs he took four mornings a week.

"We can meet in the park at eight," he said after a moment.

"Great."

Her smile lasted until Helga arrived with their food. The cream-cheese-laden bagel beckoned. The way she swallowed before sucking in her bottom lip told him as much. Whoever had been manning the knife in the kitchen had been generous with the topping.

"Anything else?" Helga asked, her meaty hands resting on a pair of what Simon remembered a great-aunt referring to as good child-bearing hips.

No way he was going to point out that his so-called fresh fruit cup looked suspiciously like the syrup-drenched cocktail variety that came in a can.

"No. We're good."

More than half of the bagel remained when Helga brought the check. Chloe considered that a victory of the highest order. She'd actually sat on her hands to keep from finishing it off. Whatever it took, she was willing to do it. She had her eye on the prize.

"You promised me a walk," she reminded Simon.

"So I did. And I never renege on my promises," he replied. He always looked surprisingly serious when he made comments such as that, and now was no exception. "Do you have a destination in mind?"

"How about that little bookstore just off Fifth? We haven't been there in a while."

It was one of the few independent shops of its kind left in the city. And while Chloe had nothing against the big stores that held every title and obscure periodical under the sun and housed trendy cafes where patrons could get a good, if pricey, cup of coffee and read their purchases, she was especially fond of this place. It was the clear underdog. Chloe knew how that felt.

"Sure."

CHAPTER THREE

The girl most likely to obsess...

IT TOOK FORTY-FIVE minutes to get to Bendle's Books, but only because Chloe stopped to do a little window shopping along the way.

"What do you think of that dress?" she asked, pointing to a clingy black number draping a mannequin that was wand-thin and eerily faceless. She turned to Simon expectantly, only to find him frowning.

"On you?"

"No. On the mannequin. I'll be sending it to the reunion in my place," she snapped, even though she was a little more wounded than irritated by his dubious tone. It didn't help that the dress undoubtedly did look better on the faceless and tummyless dummy.

He rubbed a hand over the back of his neck. "It's kind of...revealing."

"And you think I've got a little too much to reveal at this point, is that it?"

"No, Chloe—"

"I'll be thinner by then. The reunion is six weeks

away. If I lose two—okay, more like three—pounds a week, I'll be able to pull off that dress." Especially if she threw in regular toning workouts and shape wear. She mentioned the exercise to Simon, but not undergarments, adding, "You're always after me to get healthy."

"I want you to eat more balanced meals and exercise more often. I don't think you need to lose weight, at least not by going on some kooky crash diet."

She brushed off his reply and started walking. "It's not kooky."

He fell in step beside her. "Excuse me?"

"I'm not going on a kooky diet. I plan to eat sensibly, just smaller portions, and cut out comfort food entirely."

"Entirely?" Again the dubious tone.

"Last night was it. No more mac and cheese for me and no more ice cream."

"And bagels? What about those?"

"Today was an exception. What was I to do? Helga plopped that thing in front of me. I didn't eat it all," she reminded him.

"You showed admirable restraint."

"I thought so, too."

But her restraint took another beating when they passed a pizzeria and the smell of melted mozzarella cheese and spicy Italian sausage wafted out the door along with a satisfied-looking customer. She swallowed, not out of despair, but because her mouth had actually started to water. Why couldn't broccoli smell like that?

"Maybe at the bookstore I'll be able to find a cookbook

that includes some of my old favorites, just with a lot less fat and fewer calories and carbohydrates."

It was a tall order, to be sure. But hope sprang eternal.

"You could just log on to the internet, you know. A couple of keystrokes and thousands of recipes would be at your disposal."

He would know, tech geek that he was. Chloe shook her head. "I like books. I like holding them in my hands and flipping through the pages. Besides, when I download free recipes from the internet, I don't get to see Millicent."

Millicent Cox owned Bendle's. Although her daughter was largely in charge of the quaint little store these days, Millicent was a fixture behind the counter on weekend mornings.

"She's a character." He said it with fondness, rather than with the snarkiness that Chloe's last boyfriend had injected into the simple statement.

Millicent was pushing eighty and had as many stories to tell as she had obscure books to sell. Between her eclectic title selection, which included some rare editions that appealed to collectors, and a colorful past that allegedly included a turn as CIA mole, visiting her shop was always an adventure.

The older woman greeted them with a shaky wave when they entered to the jangle of cowbells.

"I haven't seen either of you in here in a while."

"Worried about us?" Simon asked on a smile.

"Not in the least." She cackled at his fallen expression,

before admitting, "Okay, maybe a little. You get to be my age and your social calendar tends to include a lot of funerals. It's easy to think the worst when you haven't heard from someone in a while."

Chloe forced a smile. Millicent didn't seem to notice.

"So, what have you kids been doing to keep yourselves busy?" the older woman asked.

"The usual," Simon replied on a shrug.

"That means he's working too many hours," Chloe clarified.

"And you?" Millicent asked.

"Not enough."

"Still part-time, hmm?"

Chloe nodded. She'd been part-time at the graphic-design company where she'd been working for the past three years, which meant she had to supplement her income by doing freelance work. It was far from ideal, but her boss kept assuring her she would become full-time soon.

"What about your love lives?" Millicent asked shamelessly. "Anything of interest to report in that area? And be generous with the details. I'm an old woman who spends all of her evenings alone. Vicarious living is the only thing I'm capable of at this point in my life."

"Sorry." Chloe shrugged. "I'm still dateless."

"Still? Heavens, it's been months," Millicent remarked, sounding horrified.

The older woman's tone, so similar to that of Chloe's mother's and the happily married Frannie, had her blurting out, "Well, Simon got dumped yesterday."

"I didn't get dumped." To Millicent, he said, "My girlfriend and I reached a mutual decision not to continue our relationship."

The older woman waved one thin, blue-veined hand in his direction. "It's the same thing, my dear."

When Chloe giggled, Simon shot her a black look.

Millicent was saying, "Workaholics make lousy mates, Simon. I found that out the hard way with husbands one through four."

He blinked in surprise. "You were married four times?"

"Five. Only the first four were workaholics. Unfortunately, I was a slow learner." She winked from behind a pair of thick bifocal lenses. "What can I say? I was a sucker for a pair of broad shoulders and a firm behind."

Chloe was past the point of being shocked by Millicent's unexpected bluntness. So was Simon.

"I'm not a workaholic," he protested.

Chloe disagreed silently. He spent too many hours at the office. It wasn't all the fault of the upcoming acquisition. He'd come far enough that he could give others in his employ more of the responsibility.

She couldn't help noticing that he also had a pair of broad shoulders and a rather fine backside.

He was saying, "As the head of the company I have a lot of responsibility, especially right now. There's a lot going on that requires my attention."

"Delegate, young man. Delegate."

Exactly, Chloe wanted to shout.

"The relationship wasn't going anywhere," he muttered. "It pretty much had run its course."

"Regardless, life is too short. It passes you by quickly. Believe me. Before you know it, you'll be worrying about hip fractures, misplacing your dentures and dozing off during the evening news." A sigh rattled out. But then Millicent offered a crafty smile. "Besides, you'll never turn the head of the girl of your dreams if you keep long hours at the office and spend your free time with women who are more interested in your title and looks than what's behind both."

Chloe felt her skin prickle.

Simon leaned one of his broad shoulders against the cash register. "You know, if you'd agree to marry me, Millicent, I'd agree to work reasonable hours, not to mention forsake all others."

"I'd be tempted to take you up on that, but I think all three of us would be disappointed." Her gaze shifted to Chloe and she smiled. "Don't you, Chloe?"

Chloe shook her head. No matter how many times they'd tried to tell Millicent that they weren't anything more than friends, the older woman kept insisting and insinuating they were or someday would become something more.

Silly, Chloe thought.

Surely, if Simon were interested in her as anything more than a pal, he would have made it clear by now. Not that she wanted him to. Or that she was interested back, despite those odd tingles she sometimes got when they were together. No. They were friends. Pals. Buds. BFFs.

She was as surprised as Millicent and Simon when a wistful sigh escaped.

Chloe cleared her throat. "I'm looking for a cookbook."

"Well, you know where to find them, my dear. The shelf by the window has some vintage ones."

"She wants one with low-carb, low-calorie recipes," he said, his bias obvious.

Millicent's mouth puckered in distaste. "The trendy ones are on the next shelf over."

Simon went with Chloe and helped her leaf through the limited selection. She settled on one that boasted nutritious meals in thirty-minutes or less. The pictures looked appetizing, the recipes didn't appear too difficult and the ingredients weren't something she'd have to hit specialty stores to find. Portion control would be the key, though. She'd learned that with the first batch of low-fat cookies she bought. Low-fat or not, it turned out that when a person ate the entire box in one sitting, the calories still wound up going straight to her hips.

"All set?" he asked.

"Just one more thing." She started for the back of the store and a section in which she had spent way too much time over the years.

"What are you doing in the self-help aisle?"

"Looking for, well, a way to help myself," she quipped.

"What book are the talk-show gurus pushing this week?" he asked in a weary tone.

"They aren't pushing anything."

One of Simon's eyebrows rose.

"Okay, so one of the guests on a show I caught last week mentioned a book that sounded sort of interesting."

"I'm almost afraid to ask, what's the title?"

She had to clear her throat before the words "*The Best You, Ever*" made it past her lips. She doubted he would care that the subtitle was "From the Inside Out." She couldn't be sure, but she thought she heard him swear. And his expression made his disdain plain.

"You're already the best you that you can be, Chloe."

Her heart did a funny somersault at his assessment, as off base as she knew it to be. She was a far cry from the person she wanted to be, especially physically, which was her main objective now with the reunion fast approaching.

"You're just saying that because you're my friend." *Pal. Bud. BFF.*

He folded his arms across his chest. "And if I wasn't your friend? Would you believe me then?"

"Simon," she began patiently.

But his tone was impatient and surprisingly irritated. "Answer me. What will it take for you to finally accept that you don't need improvement? If that last loser you dated had said so, would you have believed him?"

Whoa, whoa! Her mouth went slack.

Loser? That was cold. Okay, so she'd called Greg a loser, too, not to mention a couple dozen other choice names in the weeks following their breakup. But Simon hadn't seen the need to malign Greg's character then, other than to say the guy wasn't good enough for her. She'd been well into a pint of mint chocolate chip ice cream at the time. Simon had taken away her spoon, made her dress in something other than sweats and had taken her out to a fancy restaurant for dinner.

"This is how you deserve to be treated," he'd said at the end of the evening.

It dawned on Chloe then. Simon had never maligned the character of any of the guys she'd dated. Never... until just now.

He was joking. He had to be.

She waited for humor to leak into his expression, for the corners of his mouth to quirk in a well-remembered smile. But a full minute ticked past and Simon remained stoic, his countenance as unyielding as that of a tombstone.

"What do you want me to say?" she asked at last.

"I want you to say that you believe me when I tell you that you look fine just as you are."

"I do believe you," she assured him.

Well, sort of. Mostly. But he was her friend, her pal, her bud and BFF. People with those titles were known to lie. Which was why on days when Chloe was feeling particularly insecure about her body, she peppered Simon with questions such as, "Do these pants make my butt look big?"

No woman in her right mind asked that question of someone they thought might actually tell them the truth. Besides, the man regularly dated lingerie models.

He squinted sideways at her. "You do?"

She nodded to add emphasis. "Of course, I do." All the while, she was thinking, he had to be lying.

The rigid set of his shoulders relaxed fractionally. Simon really did have nice shoulders and the cotton pullover he was wearing did them justice. It was just snug enough to show off some of the definition that his regular workouts had created.

"Mmm."

His brows tugged together. "Chloe?"

Good God! What was she thinking? Bad, bad Chloe.

"Hmm. I said, hmm. You know, it's a kind of humming sound that can be taken for, um, well, an affirmation." Or the prelude to an orgasm. Though she was barely managing to tread water, she decided to dive in again. "As in, I believe you when you say that I look fine."

He exhaled and the beginning of a smile lit his face. "So, we can go now?" he asked.

"Yes. Right after I pick up that book."

Just that fast, he was frowning again. "But you just said that you believe me."

"And I do. I know I look fine." And, gee, could there be a more tepid word in the English language to describe one's looks? *Fine* made *plain* seem almost like a compliment by comparison. "For the reunion, I want to look spectacular."

She rolled the *R* at the end to give the word its due. His eyes pinched closed for a moment. When he spoke, his words came out clipped.

"You already do."

"No, Simon. You yourself just said I look *fine. Fine* is a far cry from spectacula*rrrrr.*"

When she turned to browse the books, he exhaled sharply and she heard something extra slip out. This was no petty potty oath like the last time she'd thought she'd heard him cut loose. Nope, this was the mother of all bad words—the very one for which his own mom had washed out his mouth with a ghastly lavender-scented bar of soap when they were in fifth grade.

She turned back. "Did you just…swear?"

"Why would I swear? What reason, Chloe McDaniels, would I possibly have to swear?"

She knew a trap when she heard one. God knew, her mother had laid enough of them during her teen years.

"Simon?" She eyed him in confusion, not at all sure why he was suddenly so mad.

He presented her with his profile and the silence stretched. Just as it was becoming awkward, he plucked a book from the shelf and held it out to her. "*The Best You, Ever.* Knock yourself out."

His smile was forced, but she didn't comment on it. In truth, she wasn't sure what to say. Millicent was still perched on her high stool behind the counter.

"What's this?" the older woman asked as she rang up the sale. "Another self-help book? What did I tell you when you purchased the last one?"

"You, too?"

Millicent frowned.

"Chloe needs more improvement," Simon said. "She

wants to be spectacular*rrrrr* for our ten-year high school reunion."

Okay, the rolled *R* just sounded ridiculous when he did it.

"A class reunion, hmm?" Millicent's smile was both sad and knowing. "I've gone to every one and can tell you I don't know why I bother."

"Why do you say that?" Chloe asked.

"I don't care about any of those people, well, except for the friends I had, and I keep in touch with those on my own. The ones who are still living, anyway."

Simon grunted.

"The others," Millicent was saying. "They're still keeping score."

Simon was nodding, feeling validated, no doubt.

Don't ask. Don't ask. Don't ask. Chloe told herself. Out of her mouth came the words, "What do you mean?"

"Well, at the tenth, it was about being married. Not many of us were career women back then. Even if we went on to college, the goal was an *M-R-S* degree. I'd already walked down the aisle twice." Her lips pinched into a frown. "Didn't score me any points, believe me.

"At the twentieth, the gossip was over who was divorced or having an affair." Millicent cleared her throat. "My ears burned all night.

"At the twenty-fifth, the talk was all about what colleges our children had been accepted to or were attending, or who they were marrying. At the thirtieth, tongues were wagging over who still looked the best."

"It took till the thirtieth for that?" Chloe asked before she could think better of it.

"Actually, that was a recurring theme throughout my reunions, much as it was back in high school."

"Some things never change," Simon muttered.

"Let me guess," Millicent said. "There were some girls who made your life miserable and maybe a boy or two who failed to glance your way."

"Right on the girls, wrong on the boys." Chloe shrugged. "I didn't find any of them to be all that interesting," she admitted. "They were so boring and immature. Well, except for Simon."

"Ah. So, who did you go to parties and school dances with?"

"Simon, of course."

Millicent's smile turned canny. Chloe didn't trust it. Before the older woman could say anything, she thrust her charge card into Millicent's hand.

"Put it on this, okay?"

"Delaying the inevitable?"

Millicent's question, accompanied as it was by a sly wink in Simon's direction, left Chloe wondering if she was talking about paying the bill or something else.

CHAPTER FOUR

Prettiest Smile

"WOULD YOU BRING Chloe and me some coffee?" Simon said to his secretary just before she exited his office.

It was a Monday morning, his schedule had been power-packed with back-to-back meetings, but when Carla had buzzed a moment earlier to tell him Chloe was in the reception area wondering if he could spare a moment, he'd had no problem clearing out his office and his schedule.

He needed a break, a few minutes away from the buttoned-up stiffs, many of whom were far older than he was, and who either didn't get his offbeat sense of humor or, worse, pretended that they did and laughed out of obligation.

Chloe's impromptu visit offered him the perfect excuse to end one meeting early and delay by half an hour the next one.

At least, that's what he told himself, ignoring the little pop of excitement he always experienced when she sought his company out of the blue.

"No coffee for me, thanks," she said.

"Would you prefer tea?" Carla asked.

Chloe shook her head. "They both stain my teeth."

Last week, Chloe had shown up for one of their morning runs with dazzlingly white teeth. Her smile looked fantastic—as far as he was concerned, it always had been one of her best features—but now in addition to all of the other don'ts on her long list of ingestibles, she'd added beverages that could dim her newly brightened pearly whites.

"I suppose red wine is off your list, too," he said once they were alone.

"I switched to chardonnay," she admitted. "Which pairs better with salads anyway."

He squinted at her blinding smile.

Salads were pretty much all that she was eating these days, despite his regular lectures on the importance of protein and complex carbohydrates.

"The reunion can't come soon enough," he said on a sigh.

"It can for me. I have a lot left to do."

From his vantage point, she'd already made a lot of progress. She'd dropped a couple of pounds and was definitely taking more care with her appearance. Case in point, the outfit she had on today—a flattering printed blouse and pencil skirt paired with rounded-toe flats that had a flirty little bow stretching over the vamp. Her frumpy, figure-hiding days apparently were over. She shifted in her seat, tugging at the hem of her skirt. Standing, the garment fell just above her knees. Sitting, it pulled to midthigh and posed way too much of a distraction, which was why he regretted that he'd moved to the sitting area in his office rather than staying at his desk. With a wide expanse of polished cherry between them, he wouldn't have been able to see her gorgeous legs.

"I'm thinking of having the gap between my front teeth fixed. That's why I came by today. I wanted to get your opinion."

His gaze snapped from her thighs to her mouth. She offered a toothy smile. Even so, he was sure he'd heard her wrong. "What?"

"I asked the dentist about it when I was in for the whitening treatment," she said. "They got back to me today on costs and…and, well, payment plans. My insurance won't pick up anything, since it's considered cosmetic. Same for the whitening, but that cost considerably less."

"You're getting braces?"

"Don't be silly." Her lips pursed in exasperation. It was an expression he knew well and one he was perversely fond of. For that matter, he even found it a turn-on, which was not exactly what he needed at the moment.

She was saying, "It would take months for my smile to be corrected with traditional braces. The dentist suggested porcelain veneers. I may be able to get away with only a couple, and truthfully, even that is more than I can afford. But that would fix the gap, at least. With, say, half a dozen more, the dentist says I could have a Hollywood smile."

Just what she felt she needed, apparently. But Simon honed in on one word and snorted. "Corrected? There's nothing wrong with your smile."

She did the exasperated lip purse again before opening her mouth and pointing. "I can spit a watermelon seed through this gap."

"Stop exaggerating. A sunflower seed at most. But even if you could spit a watermelon seed, so what? Lauren Hutton has a much bigger gap between her front teeth and she was a successful model."

"I'm no Lauren Hutton."

"You're absolutely right on that score. You're way better looking."

"That's so sweet," she said. But he knew her too well. The words were code for, "Yeah, right."

So, he tried again. "Why would you want to look like everyone else? Your differences are what make you who you are. Hell, they're what make you so damned hot."

His face grew warm afterward. He imagined his cheeks were turning a blotchy shade of red as they always did when he was embarrassed. It was an inherited trait passed down from his father, yet another thing to hold against the old man.

"You think I'm hot?" Of course he would have Chloe's full attention now.

Simon shifted in his seat and affected a considering pose that allowed him to obscure the lower half of his face behind one hand. Over the years, he had called her pretty and attractive and a host of other complimentary adjectives, mostly in answer to her prodding question, "How do I look?"

After the "fine" debacle at the bookstore, he'd even added *spectacular* to his repertoire. But *hot?* Never. Somehow that description seemed more personal. It seemed *too* personal. It crossed the invisible line in their relationship that kept them just friends.

Lovers found one another hot. Friends didn't, or at least they shouldn't.

He cleared his throat. "I've overheard guys talking."

"What guys?"

His plan to redirect her interest had worked. That was the good news. But now he was at a loss. He couldn't exactly name names, although that was precisely what she was expecting.

"I...um..."

"Oh, my God! I know!" She clapped a hand over her mouth. A pair of rounded eyes studied him.

She's figured it out. Simon wasn't sure whether to be relieved or sick. *She knows I'm not only lying to her right now about other guys, but that I've secretly had a thing for her for years. She's...*

"It's Trevor!"

Clueless.

"Trevor?"

"He's the guy you overheard saying I'm hot."

"Chloe—"

"Oh, my God!" She slapped the hand over her mouth a second time. Simon wanted to slap his forehead.

"He hasn't said hot in so many words."

In fact, Chloe's name had never come up in any of their conversations, and why would it? Despite her recent nagging of Simon to introduce her and the lawyer who was helping handle the acquisition of a smaller competitor, he hadn't.

Trevor was a nice enough guy. He played a decent game of one-on-one basketball and could talk trash with the best of them. And he was good at his job. Top-notch, in fact. He'd come on the highest recommendation and with a boatload of experience and credentials, including a Harvard law degree and five years as a junior partner at one of Manhattan's biggest firms. But he was a player.

Simon had figured that out during their first lunch together, when the guy had flirted shamelessly with their waitress, gotten the young woman's telephone number, even though he'd told Simon he had a date that evening. Since then, he'd seen the guy leaving the building with half a dozen other women, each one more lovely than the last.

Player. Definitely.

No way was Simon going to introduce someone like him to a woman as sweet and trusting and terminally romantic as Chloe.

"But are you saying he's interested in me?"

"Chloe, he's interested in everything with two legs and a pair of breasts," Simon said in exasperation.

"You're just being overprotective."

Forget terminally romantic, the woman was terminally dense when it came to men who were all wrong for her.

"So, when are you going to introduce us?"

When hell freezes over. But Simon said, "He's been out of the office a lot lately. Off in a former Soviet country, doing some work for another client. I'm not sure when he'll be back. It could be weeks."

Carla came to the door then. His secretary had foul timing. "Trevor is here."

Simon worked up a smile. "Gee. Back from Uzbekistan already?"

Carla frowned in confusion, but didn't challenge him. Rather, she said, "Apparently he didn't get the email I sent about delaying the next meeting." She glanced in Chloe's direction. "Will you be much longer?"

"No."

"Actually, we're finished." Of course, Chloe would say that. Of course she would hop up with a smile on her face, all talk of veneers forgotten, when the man entered the office.

"Sorry," Trevor said when he spied Chloe. "I didn't realize I was interrupting something personal."

"Personal? No way." This from Chloe, whose whitened teeth were blinding now. "I just dropped in to chat with Simon. He and I are old friends." Was it his imagination, or did she place way too much emphasis on the words *old friends?* "I'm Chloe McDaniels."

She stuck out her hand, which Trevor shook, a smile

spreading across his face like an oil spill. "I'm Trevor Conrad. It's nice to meet you."

"Likewise. I'm sure I'll see you around."

"A man can hope."

Simon felt his blood pressure spike. His face probably was turning blotchy again, this time from irritation rather than embarrassment. Chloe's expression was rhapsodic. This was exactly what he didn't want to happen.

"I'll walk you to the elevator," he told her as he grabbed her arm just above the elbow. "Be back in a minute, Trevor. Have Carla get you a cup of coffee."

Wouldn't it just figure that the man said, "No, thanks. I'm cutting back on coffee. It stains my teeth."

In the hall, Chloe sighed. "Can you believe that? We have something in common."

Simon thought his head would explode. Before he could get a handle on either his emotions or his tone, he snapped, "You can't really be interested in him."

"I don't want to marry him and bear his children, but sure, I'm interested. A nun would be interested."

His heart sank, weighted down with an emotion he refused to admit might be jealousy let alone something more damning. "He's a player, Chloe."

"I know that."

"You do?"

"I'm not a complete idiot, Simon. But player or not, the girls at the reunion would eat their hearts out if I showed up with him."

His blood pressure dipped a little, although not nearly enough. "So, your intention is just to use him?"

"Don't worry." She patted Simon's cheek. "I promise I won't hurt him. I'll leave him heart-whole and capable of performing his job here for you."

Simon snagged the hand that had just patted his face and pressed it tight against his heart. "I'm not worried about Trevor. He can take care of himself. I'm worried about you. I don't want to see you hurt. By him. By anyone."

She blinked, swallowed. "You're serious."

"Never more so."

He leaned forward, intending to kiss her cheek, but his mouth came to rest against hers. He'd kissed her before, hundreds of times. On the cheek. On the forehead. He'd even kissed the back of her hand in a gallant gesture that had been completely wasted on her since she was still loopy from laughing gas after having her wisdom teeth pulled. But he'd been careful not to kiss her on the lips. For this very reason. They were way too tempting.

The moment lengthened.

The dinging from the elevator just before its doors opened was what snapped him back to his senses. He pulled away, but slowly. And he could have sworn Chloe leaned after him before righting herself and offering up an uncertain smile that showed that sexy little gap.

"Don't change that," he said softly. His raised one hand and cupped the side of her face. "Don't change anything."

* * *

Don't change anything.

Simon's words echoed in Chloe's head long after they parted ways. True, he'd said those words or ones with a similar meaning dozens of times, especially recently. But hearing them had never had quite the effect they'd had on her today. He'd sounded so adamant and sincere. He'd looked so…well, gorgeous. And when he'd kissed her…

It was just a kiss, she reminded herself. A friendly peck that she was blowing out of proportion. Except, friendly pecks were usually on the cheek and the giver didn't linger and pull back slowly, almost as if in regret. Nor did the receiver of such a peck lean forward, disappointed to find the contact ending and wishing, foolishly, that it could last and turn into something more.

"I'm making too much of it," she said aloud. "He didn't mean anything by it."

The suit-clad man seated across the aisle from her on the subway train didn't so much as bat an eye. This was New York, after all. People here were used to other passengers having conversations with themselves.

But Chloe still felt like an idiot. And not only because she had an audience. This was Simon she was thinking about.

Back at her apartment, she spent the better part of the afternoon pacing and fretting even though she had some freelance work to do. She couldn't concentrate. She couldn't think. Finally, she couldn't stand it. Just after six o'clock, she dialed Simon's number.

"It's me. Chloe," she added needlessly after he

answered. He had caller identification on his telephone. And it wasn't as if her voice had changed over the past several hours, even if it seemed something had.

"Hi. This is a surprise."

"Why is it a surprise? I call you all the time. Well, not all the time, but often. And you call me." Though he hadn't tonight, and, frankly, she'd expected him to. She'd expected some sort of explanation.

"I meant, a *pleasant* surprise."

Her pulse perked up a little, which she both anticipated and found ridiculous. "I hope I didn't throw your schedule off by stopping by your office earlier."

"Believe me, I welcomed the excuse to spend a few minutes not looking over documents."

"Oh. Good. And I appreciate your advice on the veneers."

"Does that mean you're going to follow it?"

"I'm still thinking."

He made a humming noise. "So, is that the only reason you called?"

"No." Her heart knocked out a couple of extra beats. "I was just wondering…" *Why did you kiss me like that? Why did you stop? Did you feel all woozy and confused afterward, too?* Since she couldn't bring herself to ask any of those questions, she finished with "—how your day went. The rest of it. You know, after the elevator when, um, when I left."

"The rest of my day." He sighed heavily. "In a word, *lousy.*"

"I'm sorry to hear that." And she meant it, even if misery did love company.

"Want to know why?" he asked. It was issued like a dare.

Chloe swallowed and in a voice barely above a whisper asked, "That kiss?"

"I didn't hear you."

She chickened out. "I said, merger giving you fits?"

"Yeah. The damned merger." His tone turned wry. "Among other things."

"Like who? Er, I mean, what?" She wasn't being nosy. They often traded bad-day stories. She reminded him, "I'm a good sounding board. You can tell me anything."

"I know I can." But she got the distinct impression that he was holding out on her now, even though he said, "You had it right the first time. It's more like who."

Chloe knew that tone. "A woman?"

"Got it in one."

An assortment of confusing emotions nibbled around the corners of her curiosity. The one that gave her pause was betrayal. "I didn't realize you were seeing someone again."

"We're not dating." He sounded weary.

"Yet?" Chloe prompted.

"Ever."

"Why? What's wrong with her?" she asked.

"Nothing's *wrong* with her."

Chloe didn't care for the way he leaped to the woman's defense.

"Something's got to be wrong with her if she's not interested in you."

"You think?" He sounded amused now.

"She must be an idiot."

"She can be a little clueless at times," he agreed on a laugh. "In an adorable sort of way."

Uh-oh. Adorable? Chloe didn't like the sound of that. He'd never been interested in a woman he'd considered adorable. Gorgeous, sexy, sophisticated and exotic... sure. "Have you two known each other long?"

He took his time answering. "Sometimes I think maybe too long."

"Then why is this the first I'm hearing of her?" she demanded.

That odd feeling of betrayal niggled again. This time, she told herself she understood its source. Simon had always been forthcoming about the women in his life. Not that he provided intimate details, but Chloe always knew when he was involved or interested in becoming involved. So, how had she missed this one?

"It doesn't matter. Forget I mentioned it. She's...not my type," he said.

"Okay. But you're interested?"

"Forget it, Chloe. Please."

Still, she couldn't resist saying, "A bad girl, huh? The kind who wears black leather, has major body art and piercings in places that make me shudder?"

"No." But he chuckled, letting her know that as off base as she might be, at least she'd lightened his mood.

Or she thought she had.

"Let's just drop it, okay?" She heard him sigh and imagined him sinking into the cushions of the supple leather recliner in his living room.

If he swiveled around in the chair, he had a stunning view of the city out the wall of windows that faced the park. He had a killer apartment. It was three times larger than hers was, and she didn't need to be an expert on Manhattan real estate to know it had cost him a pretty penny. It fit his success, as did his tailored suits, sports car and choice tables at the city's nicest and priciest establishments. Yet Simon didn't mind, indeed, he seemed almost to prefer, spending time in Chloe's dive of a walk-up eating pizzas or Chinese takeout.

Which gave her an idea.

"I'm thinking of calling Fuwang's to place an order for Happy Family." The seafood dish was a favorite of both of theirs. "You want to come over? My treat?"

It would give her an opportunity to grill him about this mystery woman and to, well, get over this latest silly bit of interest in him that she had going.

"What happened to your diet?" Simon asked.

"Oh. Yeah. That." Her stomach growled, and no wonder. Not only was she starving, Fuwang's made some of the best Chinese food in all of Manhattan. "I can afford to splurge a little. I've eaten light all day."

"How light? I'm telling you, Chloe, you'll keel over in a dead faint if you skimp too much. Remember what I said about healthy snacks."

Grazing, he called it. The idea was to eat several small servings of nutritious food throughout the day.

Unfortunately, the word *grazing* conjured up the image of a cow in Chloe's mind, and that was not exactly the kind of mascot a chronic dieter such as herself wanted to have.

Still, Simon's obvious concern for her well-being was touching. Her boss wouldn't have cared if her current diet regimen involved regular purging as long as it didn't interfere with her productivity. Helga at Filigree's was only interested in selling more bagels. Her parents just wanted her to catch a man's eye so that she could settle down and give them more grandchildren. And then there was Frannie.

Whenever Chloe talked to her sister these days, Frannie's only question was about the scale's reading. In truth, Chloe didn't know. For that matter, she didn't have the nerve to find out, since looking at a number on a scale was the kind of downer that typically sent her into binge-eating mode. So, she was going by how her clothes fit. And they were definitely hanging a little looser these days. Yesterday, for instance, she hadn't had to lie on her bed in order to get her favorite jeans over her hips. Now, that was measurable progress.

Frannie didn't see it that way. Chloe's slim-hipped, narrow-waisted sister never had experienced a weight problem. Even after popping out two perfect children, she'd returned to a lithe one hundred and twenty pounds within mere weeks. Frannie's secrets? In addition to being rather apathetic when it came to food, spinning class and yoga. A few years back, Chloe had tried yoga at her sister's insistence. It only took one downward dog for her to sustain a minor head injury and take out the woman on the mat next to her. The instructor had refunded Chloe's money in full and begged her not to return. When asked about their relationship, Frannie claimed they were distant cousins...several times removed. They might as well have been, given their different body shapes and metabolisms.

"So, Chinese?"

"It's tempting," he admitted.

"But?"

"I'm tired, Chloe."

"Oh." A curious ache formed in her chest. "Another time, then."

CHAPTER FIVE

Best Body

SIMON MANAGED TO avoid Chloe for the rest of the week. Not seeing her was torture, but then seeing her would have been, too…after that fleeting kiss.

He'd needed to be sure that the next time they were together all of the wayward emotions he'd been experiencing were corralled back in place. So, he'd canceled a couple of running dates, claiming his work schedule was the culprit.

But now it was the weekend, and his excuses had run dry. Besides, he missed her.

She was waiting for him at their rendezvous point in the park, already stretching when he arrived. Her pose nearly had him turning around. A pair of gray jersey cotton shorts were pulled snug across her rounded bottom as she loosened her muscles. Her backside was definitely more toned than it used to be.

It was his moan that caught her attention. She turned around and offered a tentative smile. A week ago, her face would have split into a wide grin. Now they stood at arm's length in awkward silence. This, Simon told himself, was exactly what he didn't want. He recalled how things had become between him and his stepmother after she'd announced plans to divorce his father.

"Nothing will change between us, Simon," she'd assured him.

But once the divorce was final, their relationship became more and more strained. She still loved his father and now that Sherman had moved on to the woman who would become the third Mrs. Ford, Clarissa gradually stopped coming around. Simon was practically an adult by then, but he'd missed her. He wouldn't let romance botch up things between him and Chloe.

"I was worried you weren't going to be able to make it again," she was saying.

"Running a little late this morning," he lied. "Sorry about that."

"It's okay. I've just been stretching."

"Yeah. I saw." He cleared his throat and said the first thing that came to mind. "Great weather for a run."

Her brows tugged together and no wonder. Though it was barely nine, it was already pushing eighty and the air was dense with humidity.

"Just kidding." He forced a laugh. "Ready?"

They started out at a leisurely pace. As always, they were in sync. She matched his strides perfectly, one long leg kicking out in unison to his.

"I've missed you," he said. To make the statement a little less damning, he added, "Our runs are a highlight of my day."

She glanced sideways. "I've missed you, too. And, I've been worried."

"About me?"

"I think that woman has gotten under your skin. You're not acting like yourself."

Understatement of the year. "I've been busy."

"Is that all?"

It was the perfect opportunity to mention that kiss and...what? Apologize? Explain? No, the less said on that subject the better.

"It's my dad," he told her. It wasn't a complete fabrication.

"Your dad? Is he okay?"

"Actually, he's lost his mind." At Chloe's puzzled expression, Simon clarified, "He's getting married again."

Her lips formed a silent O. Then, "Does this make number six or seven?"

"Six, I think. I've lost count."

Simon sped up. Chloe matched his stride. She had long legs and was putting them to good use. He heard her breath chuffing in and out, the sound rhythmic and, in a way, comforting. He liked having her beside him.

"Sorry." He knew that she meant it. She was the only one who understood how deeply the revolving door of stepmothers in his life had affected him. "Wh-when is the w-wedding?" she asked, getting winded.

"This afternoon."

He told himself to slow down, but the demons snapping at his heels had him surging ahead. He and Chloe were in a full run now on a path dotted with other joggers and walkers. They wove in and out of the pedestrian traffic. Talking was impossible. Chloe remained at his side for a good two minutes before starting to fall behind. Little by little, his lead lengthened. He could no longer see her from the corner of his eye. When he finally stopped, it took her a moment to catch up. They stood together, panting. Both of them were bent at the waist with their hands braced on their thighs.

When her breathing somewhat returned to normal, she asked, "Feel better?"

He knew what she meant. "Not really."

"So, back to your dad's wedding, did you just learn about it?"

He straightened and pushed the damp hair back from his forehead. "I've known for a few months."

"Why haven't you said something to me before now?" She looked hurt. "First you're keeping secrets about a woman and now this? And then that—"

"That what?"

"Never mind." But he knew she was thinking about the kiss. "You're not acting like yourself, Simon."

He ignored the comment. "I figured she'd bail on my father before now. If she's smart, she'll leave him at the altar before saying 'I do.'"

"Are you going?"

He shrugged. "I thought about skipping it, but Dad asked me to pick up the ring from the jewelers, so I'll be there."

"Alone?"

"Are you offering to go with me?"

Simon hadn't planned to invite anyone. The event was akin to a dental visit, uncomfortable but necessary. But he wouldn't mind the company. Especially Chloe's.

"Of course, I'll go with you."

"Thanks."

Perspiration dotted her skin and her hair was staging an all-out revolt. He wanted to kiss her again, maybe even up the ante from the last time.

Which was why he said, "You know, I've been thinking that I'd like to host a small cocktail party at my apartment next weekend, mostly people from the office but a few friends, as well."

He'd come up with the idea the night after the kiss while he'd lain awake feeling restless and desperate. A cocktail party would allow Simon to fulfill his promise to Chloe regarding Trevor, and as such it might help restore to normal his and Chloe's just-friends status.

Two birds, one stone and the only casualty would be Simon.

"Such as me?" she asked.

He forced a smile. "It will give you an opportunity to talk to Trevor and you might consider it a dress rehearsal of sorts for the reunion, since some of the people from the office can be every bit as snobby and boorish as the Unholy Trinity."

"You'd do that for me?"

"You'll have to help Mrs. Benson with the planning," he said of his housekeeper.

"Thank you, Simon. I can't tell you how much I appreciate it."

Yeah? So why was she frowning? Sometimes he thought there was no figuring out the woman.

They finished their circuit of the park on a leisurely jog. Chloe was grateful for the less hectic pace, even if she understood why Simon had sped up. And she ached for him. As annoying as her family could be, at least they stuck around, unlike Simon's mother and favorite stepmother. And while Chloe's parents' marriage was far from ideal, beneath the nitpicking and bickering, she knew her mother and father would stick together till the end.

Perhaps because of Simon's experience, she'd never taken that kind of permanence for granted.

They arrived at the same park entrance where they'd started an hour earlier. She couldn't wait to peel off her damp clothes and stand under the cool spray of her shower.

"I think I lost five pounds in water weight," she commented.

"Same here."

Beside her, Simon tugged his drenched T-shirt over his head, exposing the kind of physical perfection his clothes only hinted at. Chloe swallowed a wolf whistle before it could escape.

Check out those abs!

How was a woman not supposed to gawk? She tried

her best to look elsewhere, but time and again her gaze returned to his defined chest and chiseled abdomen.

"You're so…"

His brows rose as he waited for her to continue.

"Lucky." She managed after clearing her throat. "You can take off your sweaty shirt in public and no one cares."

"If you want to lose yours, you won't hear me complaining." He'd said similar stuff to her before, but this time, even though he'd grinned afterward, her pulse began to rev like it had during their run. She blamed that kiss, chaste as it had been. It had her mind wandering to places where she'd previously never let it go.

"Well, I'd better head home," she said. "I have to turn from a pumpkin into something presentable for your father's wedding."

"I'll pick you up at noon."

CHAPTER SIX

Most Graceful

SIMON WAS WEARING a tuxedo when he came to collect Chloe later that day. And he arrived in a limousine rather than in his own car. The overall effect was fairy-tale-esque. No one did traditional black-and-white attire better than Simon. He had the build for it—long limbs, slim hips and broad shoulders. And he had the attitude—confident without coming off as cocky.

Indeed, he was as comfortable in formal garb as he was wearing faded jeans and a sweatshirt bearing the logo of his college alma mater. Whereas Chloe was already reminding herself to keep her shoulders back and stomach sucked in, and looking forward to the point in the evening when she could kick off her shoes. The ones she had on now were new. Already, they were killing her.

She'd never been good at walking in heels higher than an inch, but as the saying went, practice made perfect. So, she'd been wobbling about her apartment in a pair of the three-inch-high, peep-toe pumps since shortly after her shower. She'd already had to apply bandages to the back of her heels. Other blisters were forming on her toes. But she was determined to suck it up. No pain no gain and all that.

"Are you taking that, too?" He pointed to the top of her head.

With a sheepish smile she pulled the book off. It was the self-improvement one she'd purchased with him when they were at Bendle's.

"Reading by osmosis?" His lips quirked.

Actually, she hadn't gotten past the introduction, but she was determined to get her money's worth.

"Very funny. I've been practicing walking more gracefully." No small task wearing torture chambers that masqueraded as shoes.

"And the book helps?" He looked doubtful.

"If it stays on my head it means that my movements are more fluid and refined. I'm not flailing or stomping about."

"Ah. So, how many times have you dropped it?" Again his lips quirked.

"That's not the point."

The answer was seventeen, but who was counting? Well, other than her downstairs neighbor. Mrs. McNally had started banging on the ceiling with a broom handle after the fourth thud. The woman had become a bear to live above ever since she'd gotten her hearing aids fixed.

"All set?" Simon asked, consulting his watch. He

didn't look eager to be off, as much as he looked eager to have the day behind him. She understood completely.

The wedding was at a church in Connecticut with the reception to follow at a nearby banquet hall. It might be wedding number six or seven for Simon's father, but it was the first for the bride and she'd invited half the state's population. At least that's what Simon said his father had claimed.

"Just let me get my bag."

The purse was new, too, a stylish little clutch with a silver buckle. Unlike the shoes, the only pain it inflicted had been on her bank account. Forcing herself not to limp, Chloe followed Simon outside to the limo. Its uniformed driver stood at the ready with the rear door open for them.

"Thanks. I've got this," Simon told the man.

As the driver headed around to the front of the limo, Chloe said, "Wow, you went all out."

Simon sometimes relied on hired vehicles, but generally he preferred getting behind the wheel of his Mercedes.

"Actually, my father did." Simon's expression turned grim. "I think he was worried I wouldn't show up if he didn't take care of my transportation." He plucked at his tie then. "Dad paid for the tux, too."

"You look very handsome in it."

Indeed, he looked perfect. Even so, she couldn't resist fussing with his bow tie. Afterward, she glanced up and offered an embarrassed smile.

"Your tie was a crooked." By about a millimeter.

The disturbing fact was, Chloe had been looking for an excuse to touch him.

"Thanks."

"What would you do without me?" she asked on a laugh.

Despite his wry smile, he seemed utterly serious when he replied, "I hope I never find out."

Her entrance through the limousine's rear door wasn't exactly graceful or modest given the way her skirt hiked up. She tugged at the hem after settling onto the seat. Simon joined her.

"I meant to tell you earlier that your workouts are paying off."

Chloe was pleased he'd noticed, if a little embarrassed. She also felt guilty. The shape wear she'd purchased to help suck in her waist was worth every penny.

"Thanks."

"Don't mention it." He pulled at the tie she'd just straightened and his face reddened.

"Tie too tight?" she asked.

"Something's too tight," it sounded like he muttered.

Under his gaze, she started to feel warm, too. She cast about for something to say. "So, um, what's your new stepmother's name again?"

It was the wrong thing to ask. His lips curled from smile to snarl. "I think this one is Brittany, but since Dad has called them all 'Sweetheart' I'm not quite sure myself."

Chloe tipped her head to one side, but before she could say anything, he said, "Don't."

"Don't what?"

"Don't tell me to try to be happy for him."

Okay, that had been her advice the past several marriages, which might help to explain why he hadn't mentioned this one till the last possible moment. It struck Chloe then that even when Simon was in a relationship, he had always taken Chloe with him to his father's weddings.

"Maybe she's the one, Simon. Have you considered that?"

He snorted. "Please, she's twelve."

Chloe rolled her eyes.

"Okay, so she's not twelve, but damned close. She's younger than I am by a few years. It's…disturbing."

There was a definite *ick* factor there, she would admit.

"Sorry."

She reached for his hand. Simon's fingers wove through hers and their palms pressed together. Once again, she found it difficult to breathe. She forced herself to concentrate on what he was saying.

"At some point, you'd think my father would learn."

"Maybe he's a hopeless romantic," she replied, trying to be diplomatic.

"More like just hopeless." A muscle ticked in Simon's jaw, a sign that he wasn't only mad but hurt.

She couldn't blame him. His parents had divorced not long after he'd moved into her apartment building when they were kids. His mother had been the bad guy, or so Simon had thought since she'd been the one to move out and later hadn't fought for custody of her son.

"He looks too much like you," he'd overheard his mother say to his father during one of their many heated arguments before the divorce was final. "And I want no reminders of you."

That had been the first time Chloe ever saw Simon cry. He'd come to her apartment, his face ashen, his eyes swollen and red. After throwing up, he'd told her about the exchange. Then he'd fallen asleep on the beanbag chair in her bedroom.

Chloe's parents had let him stay the night.

The second and last time she saw him cry had been when his father divorced wife number two.

Clarissa had been Simon's babysitter since shortly before his mother left, which, looking back later, explained a lot of things to Chloe and shed light on the whispered conversations of some of the neighbors. But Simon had loved the woman and she'd loved him back, treating him, finally, like a child deserved to be treated by a mother. Clarissa had gone to his school functions, made a fuss over his accomplishments, arranged fun if sparsely attended birthday parties. Simon was a nerd, after all.

Clarissa had promised him that, no matter what happened between her and his father, she would always—*always*—be there for him. That's not quite how it had worked out, though.

"It's just too painful," she told him after Christmas

during his sophomore year of high school. By then, Simon's father had married wife number three.

Simon had come to Chloe's apartment once again. Sobbed as he'd sat in her bedroom. The beanbag chair was long gone, but he'd fallen asleep on the rug next to her bed. Despite the fact that Chloe and Simon were teenagers, her parents once again let him stay over. They'd been less worried about their daughter's virtue than the emotional well-being of the boy they'd long considered a son.

Recalling his pain now, Chloe asked, "I know you've said in the past that his multiple marriages aren't the reason you've never settled down, but…but don't you think they might have something to do with it?"

"Analyzing me?"

Another person might have been put off by his flinty expression. Indeed, adversaries in business probably cringed when they saw it. Chloe had grown up around it and so was immune. "Yes. So?"

"I don't want to make his mistakes," he admitted after a moment.

"You wouldn't."

"You say that with such confidence."

"And yet you don't believe me."

His response was surprisingly candid. "I'd like to."

"Simon—"

"Have I mentioned that you look lovely?"

He was trying to change the subject, but she decided to let him.

"Only once." That had been when she'd opened her

apartment door. His appreciative smile had caused her flesh to prickle. It was nice to be complimented. That was the reason behind the reaction. Which was why she said now, "Feel free to say it again."

"You do look incredible, Chloe. An absolute vision."

"What? In this old thing?" She plucked at that fabric of her new dress, but she couldn't keep a straight face.

As the car made its way through traffic, he poured two glasses of champagne and handed one to her. "Did you buy it for the reunion?"

"Our class reunion?"

"Is there another one I don't know about?"

He had her there. "No. And not exactly. I've got three contenders so far. Two still have the price tags on, so I can return them if need be."

His lips quirked. She remembered how they'd felt pressed to hers.

"Hedging your bets?" he asked before taking a sip of bubbly.

"More like my bank account," she admitted ruefully.

By the time it was all said and done, between clothes and the dentist, special diet foods and God only knew what else, Chloe was going to be out several hundred dollars.

Or more.

None of which she could afford on her current salary. Her credit cards had been inching toward their limits even before that cursed reunion invitation arrived. Her boss kept promising her a full-time position with better benefits and paid vacations, the date for which she could never pin down.

"It's the economy, Chloe," Mr. Thompson pointed out whenever she asked. "The company's bottom line has taken a real beating."

After saying this, he would grimace and turn slightly pale, making her regret having confronted him. So, she freelanced when and where she could. Even so, she never broke even, especially since her landlord had raised her rent yet again.

Simon would be appalled if he knew her true financial state. He was always after her about being prudent with her money and offering insight on smart investment opportunities. She appreciated his advice. Truly she did. And she would take it, too. Except that she never seemed to have the extra cash to spare.

Still, she considered the dresses and all of the other things for the reunion to be as smart an investment as the ones Simon had noted in the past. To her way of thinking, they would be worth the cost and then some, even if they never paid off monetarily.

Chloe needed to make a stand.

She was determined to show those horrid girls from high school that despite their nasty treatment of her, she'd turned out to be a successful, desired and appreciated adult.

Which was why it almost pained her to admit to Simon, "You'll be happy to know that I've opted not to have my teeth fixed."

To the outside observer Simon wouldn't have appeared affected by the news. Chloe knew him too well. She caught the glimmer in his eyes just before he sipped his champagne. He was delighted.

"Cloned, you mean," he said afterward.

She frowned. "Excuse me?"

"Nothing about your teeth needs to be fixed, Chloe." He shrugged. "That's why I say you were going to have them *cloned,* to look like some Hollywood starlet's."

"Whatever." She took a sip of her own beverage, not quite willing to agree with him.

"So, sanity prevailed. I hope something I said made a difference in your decision."

He could be boorish when he thought himself in the right. Still, recalling his argument now—and the kiss that followed it—warmth shimmied up her spine, every bit as effervescent as the champagne's bubbles. It caught her off guard, so much so that she spoke the truth.

"Actually, it had more to do with my bank account. Even if all I do these days is eat lettuce, I still couldn't afford it."

She laughed afterward, trying to turn her words into a joke. Simon, however, didn't share her humor. He stared straight ahead in stony silence before turning to face her.

"If you really want to have veneers put on your teeth, I'll pay for them."

Her mouth gaped open, no doubt giving him a good look at all of the dental wizardry that would be involved. "Oh, that's not necessary. I mean, I can pay for it myself."

It was a bald-faced lie and they both knew it.

"What's the latest word on your promotion to full-time?"

"Oh, you know. The economy." She shrugged her shoulders.

"I know you like your job, Chloe. And I admire your loyalty, as you know. But you need to either become more assertive or start sending out your resume. He's taking advantage of you."

"I know." She sighed.

"I'll pay for it," he said again. "If you really want those veneers, go for it."

A lump formed in her throat. It was a moment before she managed to say around it, "Why?"

"If it's important to you, it's important to me."

"After the comment you just made about cloning, you'd do that?"

"I just said I would."

"I…I don't know what to say." It was rare Chloe was struck speechless. But this was one of those occasions. Simon had been so vocal in his opposition to her getting veneers, yet now he was offering to pay for the dentist's services.

"It can be an outright gift," he was saying. "Your birthday is just around the corner." Actually, it was seven months away, but who was counting? Not Simon apparently. "Or it can be an interest-free loan if you prefer."

He'd covered all of his bases. He'd made sure that

she could choose an option that left her pride intact. Emotions swelled inside her so intense that for just a moment she had to turn her head, look out the window and battle back tears.

"Chloe?"

"The bubbles from this champagne, they're making my eyes water," she lied. She gazed into the face she knew almost as well as she knew her own. "Thank you for your kind offer, but my answer is no."

"No?" He seemed surprised.

Oddly, she wasn't, even though mere days ago she would have considered selling her soul to the devil to swing the cost of those veneers. "I've reconsidered."

"Yeah?"

"Yeah." She nodded. "You know, you're right."

How perverse, but she loved the sound of his dry chuckle just before he said, "I don't hear that often enough from you."

"Do you want to hear this or not?" she challenged.

"Oh, definitely. Go on."

"I rather like my unconventional smile. It's got... character."

"I like it, too."

He reached for her chin and pretended to examine the smile in question. She nearly started to laugh, but quickly sobered when he leaned toward her. For just a moment she thought... Nah. Ridiculous, she chided when he pulled away. He hadn't been going to kiss her.

* * *

Damn. He'd come close to kissing her again. It was going to be a very long day if every time he turned around he found himself tempted to pull her into his arms and bare his soul.

He needed her in his life too much to ever risk losing her. Friends stayed friends. Lovers…even the best of them parted ways eventually. And, when their feelings ran deep, they parted with enough acrimony to keep them from ever speaking again.

If it had been up to him, Simon would have made a perfunctory visit at the wedding reception and called it good. As far as he was concerned, his father's multiple marriages made a mockery of the institution.

But his father had ensured he would be there for the duration by tapping Simon as his best man, a fact Simon didn't know until he showed up at the church, ostensibly to deliver the ring his father had asked him to collect from the jewelers the week before.

He walked out of the back room the groomsmen were using to prepare for the ceremony and sighed with relief when he spied Chloe. She was standing next to a large potted palm tree, looking furtively about as she divested herself of her heels. He'd wondered how long she would last in them. In the choppy wake of his father's emotional ambush, the usual humor Simon would have found in the situation was lacking.

When he reached her, she asked, "What's wrong?"

He unclenched his jaw. The words that spilled out of his mouth were no less bitter. "You know how my dad asked me to pick up the ring for him?"

"Uh-huh. Saved him a drive into the city you said."

"Yeah. That's what I thought when I agreed to do it." He plucked at his pleated shirtfront. "And this tuxedo and the stretch limo…"

"Hedging his bets," she said slowly.

"Exactly. He wanted to be sure I'd be here today. On time and dressed the part."

She frowned. "The part? What do you mean?"

"I'm the best man." Simon swore afterward, soft enough that he couldn't be overheard by anyone but Chloe.

And God.

He scrubbed a hand over his face. Here he was, in church of all places, and he'd let loose with a prime curse. It just went to show that, as always, Sherman Ford had a knack for bringing out the worst in his only child.

"Best man, hmm." Chloe whistled through the slim gap in her teeth. "I guess he really was hedging his bets."

"He set me up."

"Yes."

"He manipulated me."

"He was worried you would say no," she said softly.

"That's because I would have. I've told him no ever since I was the best man at his second wedding." Simon had been a boy then, still wounded from his mother's abandonment and so damned idealistic that he'd actually believed his father's second stab at "until death do us part" would hit the mark.

"So, what are you going to do?"

He wasn't one to make snap decisions, but he made one now, eschewing manners or protocol or whatever else a situation such as this demanded in favor of righteous indignation. "I'm going to leave. Put your shoes back on. We're out of here."

She slipped her feet back into the pumps, not quite able to camouflage her wince as she did so. And, yes, he'd noticed the bandages she'd applied where blisters had started to form. Another time he would have teased her about them. Right now, he was too focused on his anger.

"You can't just leave."

"Watch me. To hel..." He glanced around, half expecting to catch the glint of a lightning bolt. Hastily, he amended, "To heck with him. I didn't want to come today anyway, at least to the ceremony. It's a farce."

Simon folded his arms over his chest. He was being belligerent, borderline petulant, and he knew it. Hated it. But damn if he didn't feel like a child again, one told how to act and how to react to being manipulated by the adults in his life.

Chloe, now as back then, was the voice of calm and reason. "You're here. You're wearing the tux he paid for." She ran her fingers under the edge of the lapels. The gesture had Simon forgetting his irritation with his father for a moment. "What will it hurt to do this for him, Simon?"

He bent closer, lowered his voice, though his words came out no less vehemently. "I hate being a party to it, Chloe. Even if I'm an adult now, I hate getting to know someone, maybe even starting to like her, and then—bam! Dad or his new wife moves on to greener pastures."

He swallowed. It was a truth he wouldn't have spoken to anyone else.

Her hands were now resting on his chest. Her cheek mere inches from his mouth. A stray curl tickled his jaw and the simple scent she'd worn since high school twined around him. To anyone watching, they would appear to be a couple, lovers lost in an intimate moment. Only part of that was true. They weren't lovers, but he'd never achieved the same level of intimacy with another woman, even those women with whom he'd made love. Chloe pulled him into a hug, pressing her lips against his cheek.

Afterward, she told him, "As I said in the car, you have to go in hoping for the best. Maybe this marriage will work." She coughed delicately. "The vast differences in their ages notwithstanding."

"You don't honestly believe that?"

"For their sake, yes." She smiled. The arms that were still encircling his shoulders tightened. "You can do this. You can get through this."

The words she spoke were familiar, he realized. She'd told him the very same thing on occasions in the past when he'd found himself facing something seemingly insurmountable, whether it was finishing up an award-winning project for the annual science fair or getting his IT business off the ground on a shoestring budget just after college graduation.

"You always have faith in me."

"Of course I do." She grinned. "And, I'll be right here the whole time for support. Or to supply liquor."

Of course she would.

"You know what you are, Chloe?"

"A good friend," she replied.

She was much more than that, but he nodded. "The very best. And always grace under pressure."

She snorted at the compliment. "Don't expect any grace out of me. You'll probably have to carry me at some point. As it is, I'm already all but maimed from these shoes. And the night is young."

A moment ago Simon had longed for the day to be over. He'd wished himself to be anywhere but in this quaint church in rural Connecticut about to witness his father's latest attempt at matrimony.

But now, with Chloe at his side, the night stretching out in front of him seemed to hold much more promise.

CHAPTER SEVEN

Best Dancer

"I CAN'T SIT at the head table," Chloe hissed through a brittle smile as Simon guided her from a seat at the rear of the banquet hall to the long table at the front.

The bride didn't look happy about the arrangement, and no wonder. The symmetry of the head table was off now that the waitstaff had hastily added a place setting next to Simon's on the groomsmen's side.

"Sure you can," he told her.

"I'm not a member of the bridal party."

"I'm making you an honorary one. I have that power as the best man, you know." They reached their destination and he pulled out a chair for her. "It's one of the perks."

"It is not." But she was hard-pressed to keep a straight face.

"Sure it is. At least in my case. See, when I agreed to do this after talking to you, Dad said he owed me." Simon settled into the seat next to hers. "Well, I called in the debt."

Chloe glanced down the table and intercepted twin death stares from the young woman wearing white and the chartreuse taffeta-clad maid of honor. "The bride is not very happy."

"She'll have to get used to it. It won't be the first time she's unhappy while married to my father," he said.

"Simon, this is her day."

"I'll make it up to her with the toast," he said. "It will be inspired."

That caught her off guard. She blinked, impressed. "When did you have time to write a toast?"

Every second between the ceremony and the limousine ride to the banquet hall had been taken up by the photographer, a demanding perfectionist of a man who'd insisted on every possible shot. Bride holding flowers in front of her. Bride holding flowers slightly offside. Bride smelling flowers. Bride balancing bouquet on her nose and clapping like a seal. Well, maybe not that one, but the session had taken forever. Thank goodness Chloe had been able to sit in a church pew and remove her shoes for the duration, although it had been all the harder to stuff her feet back inside afterward. The pumps now felt about two sizes too small.

Of his toast, Simon was saying, "I haven't actually written one. But I remember bits and pieces from the ones that Dad's other best men have given over the years." He shrugged and reached for his water glass. "Change a couple of names and dates, add in a personal story or two that she probably hasn't heard and, *voila*. It will be as sweet as saccharine."

"Simon, I meant it when I said this is...um..." Bethany? Brittany? Brandie? "What's her name's day."

"Call her sweetheart," he suggested with a wink. "Or baby will do."

His sarcasm in this case was understandable. The woman was very young. In fact, Chloe wasn't sure the bride was of the legal age to indulge in the champagne she was sipping. "She's the bride. She's in love. She's dreamed of this day for a long time, making plans, picking out colors and cake designs. Under her bed, she's probably got half a dozen scrapbooks filled with pictures of wedding dresses that she's collected over the years."

Simon's brows puckered at that.

"Never mind. What I'm saying is, don't spoil this moment or this memory for her just because you're ticked off at your father."

"He'll ruin it. Maybe not today, but eventually. He always does."

"Then let him be the jerk. You don't need to be one."

Simon didn't say anything. Rather, he fiddled with the handle of his soup spoon for a moment before tapping the end against the side of his water goblet. The clanging caught the attention of the other guests. Conversations quieted as they picked up their own utensils and joined in the quaint tradition.

Simon nodded to Chloe before glancing down the table at his father.

"Hey, Dad, in case you've forgotten, this means you're supposed to kiss your bride."

Afterward, Chloe leaned over and said, "Now, *that* is true grace under pressure."

"That's only because you bring out the best in me."

A little while later, Simon gave his toast. It was simple and eloquent if not completely sincere. Only Chloe, of course, recognized the latter.

Rather than plagiarize the toasts of his father's previous best men, he said, "Someone once told me that love is a gift to be cherished. I was a kid at the time and I don't think I gave the words much thought. But as an adult, I know them to be true." He raised his glass then. "To the bride and groom and a gift to be cherished."

The room echoed with "hear, hears" and the sound of glasses clinking together.

"I'm proud of you," Chloe whispered when Simon returned to his seat.

"You should be. And thanks for the inspiration."

She frowned.

"You were the one who told me that. It was just after Clarissa left."

Ah. His first stepmother and the only real mother he'd ever known. She remembered now. Simon had vowed that he would never love or trust anyone again. Chloe had told him he wasn't being fair to himself or the other people in his life. She hadn't been quite as eloquent as he'd been just now.

As she recalled, she'd said, "It's like chocolate. I love chocolate. Last year, when I got the stomach flu, I barfed up the candy bar I'd just eaten. Now, if I'd given up chocolate after that bad experience, I would be depriving myself."

"Gee, you should work for a greeting card company," he'd replied drily.

But they'd both laughed.

"I'm glad you didn't use my analogy," she told him now.

"I thought it best not to given that we're about to eat."

"Do...do you really believe love is a gift to be cherished?"

"Yes."

"Have you ever been in love?"

He twisted the stem of his glass between his fingers. "Yes."

This was news to her and an even bigger surprise than his revelation of a mystery woman. Were they one and the same? Perhaps not since he said they'd never dated and never would. Her mind flipped through the mental index of his past girlfriends. "Who?"

"Someone really special."

He was being evasive. And she was being nosy. Even so, another question popped out. "Does she have a name?"

"Let's just call her sweetheart."

She folded her arms over her chest. "That is so unfair."

"What?"

"You know the vital statistics of every guy I've ever

fallen for, not to mention the kind and quantity of ice cream I ate after the breakup."

"You're an open book."

And he was being way too closemouthed, which wasn't like him. "A little *quid pro quo,* please."

But he sipped his champagne and remained silent.

"God! Please tell me it wasn't that horrible Daphne Norton woman."

"What did you have against Daphne?"

"She was rude, self-centered and...and a lingerie model."

Simon chuckled. "I fail to see how her being a lingerie model made her horrible."

"You wouldn't," Chloe grumbled, and since her glass was empty, she reached for his champagne. After taking a sip, she said, "Not Gabriella."

"Ah, Gabriella." He made a humming sound of appreciation. "We had some good times."

"No doubt. The woman was capable of putting both of her legs behind her head."

"Very flexible," Simon agreed with a fond smile. "She was a former gymnast, you know. Went to college on a scholarship and nearly secured a spot on the U.S. Olympic team."

Chloe's lips curled. "I didn't want to mention this, but she hit on me once."

"She did not." He took back his champagne.

"Well, not overtly, but I sensed some...vibes. I think she was only using you to get to me."

He laughed. "It's a good thing I didn't love her, then."

"So, who? It's not like you to hold out on me."

"Someone who hasn't got a clue," he said softly.

"Unrequited love," she murmured on a sigh. As romantic as she found such things in novels, she ached for her friend. At least that's what she told herself caused the twinge in the region of her heart. "I'm sorry, Simon."

"It's okay." He handed his glass back to her. "Actually, it's for the best."

"How can you say that?"

"We'll never have a chance to hurt or disappoint one another."

Over the next couple hours, dinner was served and the dishes cleared away. The cake was cut and the bouquet tossed. Chloe managed to be elsewhere during the last event. As far as she was concerned, nothing shouted desperation more than a gaggle of single women jockeying for position behind a bride, so eager to catch a bunch of wilted blooms that they would mow down anyone who stood in their way.

Chloe should know. She'd sustained bruised ribs at her sister, Frannie's, wedding after their cousin Marilyn had launched herself over the competition like a heat-seeking missile. Marilyn caught the bouquet and was spared injury thanks to a soft landing…on Chloe.

The incident was family lore now and preserved for succeeding generations thanks to the video taken on a cell phone camera and uploaded to the internet. Last time Chloe had checked, it had been viewed four hundred and seventy five thousand times. She'd even been recognized on the street once by a teenage tourist, who'd pointed to Chloe and hollered excitedly to her friends, "Oh, my God! It's the woman from the Battle of the Bridesmaids video!"

The girls had actually asked for her autograph. More mortified than flattered, Chloe had signed their I Love New York T-shirts with an alias.

As she returned to the head table from her hiding spot in the restroom, the lights were lowered and the disc jockey announced the bridal dance would soon commence.

"Duty calls," Simon said, resigned.

"Where's your better half?" Chloe looked around for the maid of honor.

"Probably texting the pimply-faced kid who caught the garter to see if he wants to take her to the prom."

"She's not *that* young." Chloe slipped off her shoes on a groan. "And we're not *that* old."

"Says the woman with the arthritic feet."

She reached over and punched his arm. "They're not arthritic. They're blistered. Big difference."

He pretended to rub his biceps. "Does that mean you won't be able to dance with me tonight?"

"I can still dance."

"That's the spirit."

"Nothing fast, though," she said. Just the thought had her wincing.

"Perfect. You know me. I don't do fast. Nor does any other man who is sober and prefers not to make a fool of himself."

She laughed until she spotted a blur of chartreuse. "Uh-oh. Maid-of-honor closing in at three o'clock."

"Damn. I thought for a moment that I might be off the hook. Save me the next slow one?" he asked.

Just the thought of squeezing her sore feet back into her pumps had Chloe wincing anew. "Can I leave off my shoes?"

"Sorry." Simon's expression turned appropriately rueful. "It's the bride's wedding day. What's Her Name has been dreaming of this day for years. Everything must be perfect. Barefooted guests? That's not so perfect."

"It's all right. I know the best man." She winked. "I hear he has pull."

"Okay, but it will cost you."

"What's the going rate for a shoeless dance?" she asked.

"I'll let you know," he replied just as the maid-of-honor reached them.

He pushed to his feet and buttoned his jacket, looking handsome and sophisticated and miserable, though the latter was only obvious to Chloe. She knew that polite smile to be a fake, his polished manners a facade behind which he hid his true feelings. What's Her Name and What's Her Name's Friend, had no idea what this was costing him. But Chloe knew. And so did his father.

Sherman stopped behind her chair on his way to the dance floor. He was a big man, his build leaning more toward stocky than muscular. But he had a charming smile—it was where Simon got his—and a way with women. Another trait his son had inherited. It was hard not to like him, even if he had a lot of qualities that made him a bad father and a lousy role model.

"I wanted to thank you, Chloe."

"For what, Mr. Ford?"

"For getting Simon to do this for me today. I know he wasn't happy when I approached him about being my best man before the ceremony."

That was because he'd felt trapped and played, but Chloe kept those thoughts to herself. "Oh, I had nothing to do with it. He might have been a little upset at first." Total understatement of the year. "But you're his dad. He wanted to do this for you. He was actually looking forward to the toast," she embellished.

"You're a rotten liar, kiddo." His face split into a wide grin that took the sting out of his words.

"Okay, maybe not looking forward to it, but he… um…rose to the occasion."

Sherman sobered at that. "He certainly did. Surprised me, I have to say. I was prepared for him to launch a verbal grenade or two."

"I'm sure that never crossed his mind."

"I'm sure it did." Sherman laughed again before leaning down to kiss her cheek. "So, thanks for talking him out of it." Before she could deny it, he added, "We both know you're the only person in the world my son listens to."

"Would you listen to me, already? I'm telling you, Burton Cummings was no longer with The Guess Who when he recorded 'I Will Play a Rhapsody.'"

But Simon was shaking his head before she finished. "You're wrong."

The pair of them had become fans of the Canadian singer/songwriter in high school after some students lip-synched the words to "American Woman" during a mock rock competition. They both were partial to the stuff he'd recorded as a solo artist.

"I'm not wrong," she insisted. "I can't believe the DJ has that one in his collection."

"Actually, he doesn't. But he did have another one of Cummings's songs."

Chloe's eyes narrowed. "Which…" The music started and she had her answer: "Stand Tall," a ballad about a man pining for his lost love. Cummings voice was flawless, the melody moving, but the song wasn't exactly standard wedding fare. In fact, it was downright inappropriate.

"Simon, you didn't."

"What?" He shrugged innocently. "I like this song. You like this song."

"I wouldn't say I like it," Chloe muttered. The truth was, she only played it after breakups, singing into an empty spoon between mouthfuls of ice cream.

"And it's slow," he was saying. "You said you'd dance with me. I'm even willing to protect you from the bride, since you don't want to wear your shoes."

He put out his hand. His smile was devilish, but engaging. It said, I've behaved myself enough for one night. How was she to resist? Interestingly, dancing to music more suited to a wake than a wedding wasn't the only thing Chloe found tempting once she and Simon were on the dance floor and he took her into his arms. Their bodies brushed, bumped together. They both pulled back, far enough at first that Orson Welles could have stood comfortably between them. Slowly they came back together, though a gap remained.

Her sister referred to this as the chastity gap. Frannie claimed that if a man was interested in a woman in a romantic or sexual way, he breached that gap, leaving no doubt as to his intentions for later in the evening. Of course, Frannie had been the queen of dirty dancing back in her pre-marriage days. Still, she had a point. If a man wanted a woman, he held her close. She wasn't thinking of Simon now, but the guy she'd dated three boyfriends ago. The chastity gap had showed no signs of closing the entire four months of their relationship.

"Maybe he respects you too much," had been Simon's take.

She liked that explanation far better than Frannie's, which was that the only reason he was dating Chloe was for all of the free design help she was giving him with his start-up business. She'd mocked up a few— okay, seven—promotional brochures and fliers for him. And had created a company logo and slogan. And had gotten him a deep discount at the local print shop she used. And had hooked him up with an up-and-coming webpage designer whose prices were really affordable given the quality of his work. Hmm. Now that Chloe thought about it, he'd bailed on her just after the site went live.

"You're frowning," Simon remarked. "How are your feet feeling?"

Better than her ego at the moment. She smiled. "Better now that I'm not wearing shoes."

Without the heels, her eyes were level with Simon's chin. She spied the scar just below it. A sixth-grade science experiment gone awry was responsible. He'd been lucky that the volatile mixture he'd accidentally concocted hadn't resulted in more damage to either him or his apartment when the beaker exploded. The scar was visible only at certain angles and his eyebrows had grown back nicely.

"I think my dad just saluted me." Simon was the one frowning now.

"What?" She glanced around. Mr. Ford was at the head table, grinning broadly as he sat next to his none-too-happy bride. He raised his hand to his brow again, this time apparently for Chloe's benefit. "I think he appreciates how long you've managed to behave yourself."

The song ended and another slow one began. They stayed on the floor. Most of the other young people cleared off. This song was an oldie, dating back to the days of crooners such as Bing Crosby and Frank Sinatra.

It got Chloe thinking.

"How many weeks of ballroom dancing lessons do you think it would take to have the basics down?" she asked Simon.

"I don't know. Why?"

"For the reunion, I think it would be really nice to be able to do more than turn in a circle like a drill bit."

His brows shot up. "Is that a stab at my dancing?"

"Not at all. Besides, you're not going to be my date."

The corners of Simon's mouth pulled down. "You don't know that Trevor will go or, assuming he does, that he knows how to ballroom dance."

"Good point."

"I'm still offended, by the way." He grunted. "Drill bit."

"I wasn't talking about you." She coughed. "Not directly, anyway."

"That's it." The arm around her waist tightened.

"What?"

It sounded like he said, "Prepare to be dazzled," before the hand on her hip pushed her away. She stumbled a few steps out only to find herself reeled back to him with the hand holding hers.

"Simon?"

"Shut up and follow."

No drill-bit dancing now. The style wasn't quite ballroom and definitely not salsa, but his moves were choreographed rather than random. And he executed every one of them flawlessly, even as Chloe shuffled around after him. And forget that so-called chastity gap. He'd breached it half a dozen times already, each time a little more erotically than the last.

"You've been holding out on me. When did you learn how to do this?" she asked as he guided her through a turn. It wasn't the moves that left her breathless.

"A while ago. Margo was fond of dancing."

Margo. Tall, thin, with jet-black hair and a pair of exotic green eyes. She'd been the understudy in a Broadway musical when she and Simon dated two years earlier. In addition to having the sinewy body of a ballerina, the woman sang like an angel. Chloe still wasn't sure why she'd hated her. Or, for that matter, why it had been mutual. But they'd disliked one another from the start.

"Get ready." Simon was wearing that charming, devilish grin again.

"For wha*aaaaaat?*" The word stretched until it became shrill. She couldn't help it.

One minute, Chloe was upright. The next, she was tilted back over one of his arms, far enough back that she could see the silver disco ball rotating overhead. And then Simon's face appeared mere inches from her own. They were both out of breath. From the dancing? She couldn't be sure. He wasn't smiling. Not really, even though one side of his mouth was lifted smugly. She knew he was pleased with himself. Which was why the rest of his expression was so out of place. His brows were gathered together so that a line formed between them. He seemed disoriented, as if he were the one whose world had been turned on its axis.

The song was over. An up-tempo one now played in its place. Slowly, he returned her upright. Chloe became aware of the floor filling up again around them with young people, mostly women dancing with their girlfriends. Simon was right, she thought idly. Most guys didn't like to dance fast unless they were either really good at it or really drunk. Since he was neither, it was even stranger then that they were still on the dance floor.

But, of course, they weren't dancing.

A woman bumped into Chloe from behind, causing her to stumble forward. She tried to catch herself before she could crash into Simon's chest, but she couldn't quite manage it. That chastity gap was a goner. What Chloe discovered in its place when their bodies pressed together was disconcerting.

"We probably should sit down. I don't think my bare feet are safe out here amid all these spiked heels," she told him on a forced laugh.

But it wasn't only her feet that felt vulnerable.

CHAPTER EIGHT

Most Naive

CHLOE WAS MEETING Simon for dinner. It had been his idea, but she had been planning to call him anyway and see if he wanted to cash in on that rain check for Chinese. The reason she gave was that they could go over plans for his upcoming cocktail party. Actually, she just wanted to see him. Even though only a few days had passed since his father's wedding, it felt way too long.

They'd left the reception half an hour after their dance. She'd felt light-headed, which she'd blamed on the champagne. Simon walked her to her door, as he always did. Every step of the way, her pulse had revved. Would he kiss her? Did she want him to? But he was a perfect gentleman, even if he'd hesitated for just a moment before bussing her cheek.

She went to bed that night confused and needy and a little lost. He wanted her. At least his body had told her so after their dance. What was happening between them? In the past, she would have called Simon to discuss her feelings. But how could she do that now when he was the source of them?

She took an unexpected detour on the way to the restaurant, stopping in at Bendle's Books after spying Millicent through the window. It wasn't like the older woman to work a weeknight.

"What are you doing here?"

"My daughter had a hot date and we're short-staffed tonight. So, I offered to man the counter."

"That's nice of you."

"More like crafty. She was going to cancel on him. At her age, she can't afford to be canceling dates." Millicent's eyebrows rose then and her gaze skimmed Chloe's attire. "Speaking of hot dates, where's yours?"

Knowing that Simon would be dressed in a suit since he was coming right from the office and that the restaurant required men to wear jackets, Chloe had gone with another of the dresses in the running for the reunion. It was sleeveless and black, but with a subtle print in charcoal around the hem. It looked best with the fun red stilettos she'd bought, but since the blisters on her feet hadn't had a chance to heal, she'd gone with black kitten heels.

"Oh, I'm not going on a date." Chloe waved her hand. "I'm just having dinner with Simon."

"Oh?" The older woman smiled knowingly.

"Come on, Millicent," she chided out of habit. "You know that he and I are just friends."

"I never could figure that one out." The older woman leaned over the counter. "It's just the two of us here now. You can tell me. Haven't you ever wondered what it would be like if you and Simon were more than friends?"

"No."

"So, he's like a brother to you?"

"No!" Chloe coughed.

Millicent grinned. "I thought so."

"We're just friends," she stressed.

The older woman's eyes narrowed. "Are you telling me that, in all the time you've known one another, he's never kissed you?"

"Well, sure, he's kissed me."

"I mean, the way a man kisses a woman he'd like to take to bed."

Chloe's skin prickled and the sensation was not completely unpleasant. "Millicent!"

"Oh, don't sound so shocked. I'm old, not dead. Well?"

"No. Not really." Given the gleam in the older woman's eye, Chloe regretted her slip immediately. She only succeeded in making it worse, however, when she added, "It wasn't a major kiss."

"What constitutes minor these days?" Millicent wanted to know.

Chloe had put her foot in it now, so she said drily, "The same as what did in your day, I'd imagine. This was a peck, really."

"Was it recently?"

"Last week."

"Where were you when he gave you this *peck?*"

"At his office, waiting for the elevator. I was just leaving."

Millicent looked crestfallen. "When you said minor, you weren't kidding."

"It's just that he's never kissed me on the mouth before." Nor had he ever danced with Chloe quite as he had at his father's wedding. She'd woken up more than once the past few nights, thinking of the way their bodies had fit together and the awareness that she'd felt simmering just beneath the surface. And then there was the telltale hardness she'd felt when they'd been pressed together.

It was wrong. It had to be. Yet, in so many ways, it felt so right.

"On the mouth, you say?" Millicent perked up upon hearing that.

Chloe wanted to groan. It was for her own benefit that she said, "You're making too much of this. Nothing Simon did or said was over the line. And, ultimately, the kiss was very platonic."

"You sound almost disappointed," Millicent remarked.

Was she?

"Oh, no. Why would I be disappointed? Simon and I have been friends forever. If he were interested in me that way, he would have said something long before now. Besides, the women he dates are, like, supermodels."

"So, what does that mean? You're not his type?"

She's not my type. A warning bell went off in Chloe's head. Simon had made that very comment regarding his mystery woman when the two of them had talked on the telephone the night of their kiss.

"Are you interested in him that way?" Millicent was asking.

"I never really let myself be."

"That's a curious answer. Why ever not?"

"He's my best friend. If I'm wrong, I risk not only making a fool of myself, I risk losing him."

"And if you're right?"

It was a lot to think about, unfortunately a glance at her watch revealed that she didn't have time.

When Chloe arrived at the restaurant fifteen minutes later, Simon was already seated at a table. The restaurant was a new, upscale eatery in the theater district that both of them had expressed an interest in trying. They'd sampled lots of new Manhattan restaurants together during the past decade. She'd never felt awkward about their quasi-couplehood until now. Tonight, she weighed his every gesture and expression.

He stood when she reached the table. If the maître d' hadn't pulled out her chair, she knew Simon would have performed that simple courtesy for her.

"I took the liberty of ordering an appetizer and a couple of glasses of wine. White," he said before she could protest. "And don't worry about blowing your diet. A little tomato and basil bruschetta won't kill you."

"Thanks."

"Another reunion contender?" he asked, his gaze skimming her dress.

She nodded. "What do you think?"

"I think you'd look great wearing a burlap sack, but this beats burlap hands down."

It was the sort of compliment she usually dismissed with a laugh. Tonight, her heart actually fluttered and her mouth went dry.

He apparently noticed. "I like this."

"What?"

"Your quiet acceptance of the truth for once. No arguing or brushing my words aside." He nodded. "Yeah. I definitely like this."

The waiter arrived then with their wine, which was just as well. Chloe wasn't sure how to respond without making a fool of herself.

The food didn't disappoint and neither did the ambience. Chloe couldn't help noticing that the secluded tables and low lighting were perfect for intimate conversation. As usual, she and Simon never ran out of things to say, though every now and then one or the other of them seemed to lose their train of thought. The pauses weren't unpleasant exactly, but they seemed pregnant with meaning.

The evening ended on an awkward note, too. Outside the restaurant, after he'd hailed a cab for her, he leaned in to kiss her on the cheek. They both moved in the same direction, before both moving in the other direction. Finally, he cupped her face between her hands and turned it to the side so he could buss her cheek.

They both laughed afterward. But something between them was off-kilter.

* * *

The following afternoon, Simon made it to Chloe's apartment in record time. He'd defied death and the speed limit after his secretary gave him the message that Chloe needed to see him. It was a matter of life and death.

He should have remembered Chloe's gift for hyperbole.

Still, he was enjoying the show. She was stalking around her tiny living room, an enraged goddess, with one fist raised and shaking.

"I can't believe I didn't get the mailing from the reunion committee about sending in a biography for our class booklet until today! When did you get yours again?"

"It came with the invitation."

"Which you received an entire week before I did."

"I'm sure it was an oversight."

She stopped pacing. "Oversight my... It was intentional. And now I only have one day to get it in before the deadline. How convenient is that?"

"You still have time. You can send it to them via email. The booklet doesn't go to the printer's until tomorrow."

"I need more time."

"For what? It's a biography. No more than three hundred and fifty words."

"It's our yearbook all over again."

"No."

But silently, he had to admit it was. For their yearbook, Chloe's senior portrait had mysteriously gone missing. They'd plugged in a cropped down shot of her from Spirit Week when she'd painted her face the school's colors. It wasn't her most flattering look. Under her name, in the spot used to list the accomplishments of the high school seniors, hers was left blank. No mention of her involvement in several school clubs or her honor roll ranking.

"Well, I'm not going to let them make assumptions about me. I'm going to email them a biography, and they're going to weep when they read it." She booted up her laptop, looking determined, looking lovely.

It was after ten when she finally stood and arched her back. Several vertebrae cracked. Simon, who'd drifted off to sleep, stirred. He pushed her cat off his chest and sat up.

"Are you done?"

"I am. And it's a masterpiece."

He didn't trust her smile. "Mind if I read it?"

"Sure. If you see any typos, let me know. I'm going to jump in the shower."

It was free of typos, but full of…embellishment. Heck, Donald Trump was a piker in comparison. She hadn't been commissioned to design the invitations for the mayor's inaugural ball. Nor was she responsible for new tourism brochures for Ellis Island. For that matter, she hadn't done most of the stuff she'd listed in her biography. But Simon could think of dozens of things that Chloe had left off. Things that she didn't think made her sound successful, but that in his mind spoke to her character.

Such as the pro-bono work she'd done for her favorite bookstore and the internet blog she'd set up for Helga so the woman could keep in touch with family members who were spread around remote parts of Europe.

Chloe still didn't get it. She was measuring herself by some faulty past standard, unable to see her own worth. He started typing. He finished just as he heard the shower switch off, and he was quite pleased with the result. In his mind, it truly reflected the remarkable woman she was.

He did a quick copy and paste of his version of her biography into the body of an email and sent it off to the address the reunion committee had supplied. When Chloe joined him a couple minutes later, her version was back up on the desktop.

Her hair was wet and she'd pulled on a pair of sweats he'd seen her wear a million times. She smelled of soap and inexpensive shampoo, but expensive perfumes were no more enticing. The way his body reacted upon seeing her, she might as well have been wearing lingerie.

As she dried the ends of her hair with a towel, she asked, "So, what did you think?"

His mouth went dry before it dawned on him that she was referring to the biography.

"I didn't realize you were so talented," he replied drily.

She cleared her throat. "Everybody embellishes when it comes to these sorts of things, Simon. Well, unless they're like you and have practically conquered the world before age thirty."

"You've done plenty to be proud of." He shrugged. "But I know better than to argue with you. So, I sent it."

"You did? As is?"

"As is."

He refused to feel the least bit guilty about lying.

CHAPTER NINE

Easiest to Talk To

SIMON GRUMBLED AN oath as he reached for his tie. What on earth had possessed him to offer to host a party at his apartment so Chloe could chat up Trevor with the goal of getting him to take her to the reunion?

"Because I'm insane," he told his reflection in the mirror.

He also was jealous.

He wasn't willing to admit that character defect out loud. It was hard enough to admit it to himself. He'd thought he'd dealt with his attraction to Chloe a long time ago and accepted the necessary limits that he'd imposed on their relationship. He loved her, but he would never make love to her. Or act as anything other than her longtime friend. But lately he was having a hard time not trespassing on territory that he'd deemed out of bounds.

It didn't help that Simon was between girlfriends or that ever since the invitation to their reunion had arrived, he and Chloe had been spending more time in one another's company.

Being with her was proving to be hell on his self-control. The other night was a prime example. He'd left her apartment not long after sending her biography into cyberspace. But he'd wanted to stay, and not just to watch the old Hitchcock movie she found playing on cable.

But what really concerned Simon was the way she was letting their damned reunion take over her life.

If she were anyone else, he would suggest she seek therapy or, at the very least, urge her to take up a hobby. But since Simon had been present for Chloe's high school years, with an up close and personal view of the bullying and abuse she'd endured at the hands of that brazen trio of girls, he understood what drove her. And he understood that going back, rubbing their faces in her current success, *was* her therapy.

That's exactly why he'd talked her into attending in the first place.

In that regard, he was proud of her. She was standing up for herself and willingly facing her demons. He'd always known she didn't lack nerve. Or smarts. Or anything else. She was the one with doubts.

But he wished that she would face her past just as she was, comfortable with herself, proud of the girl she'd been and the woman she had become. She didn't need to change, let alone improve. Sure, he was happy to see her eating healthier and getting more exercise. It was her motives for doing so that troubled Simon.

Just as it was his motives for throwing this party that troubled him. He was doing it for Chloe, because he was her *friend,* and yet hoping desperately that nothing would come of any flirtation that might occur between her and Trevor. That didn't exactly make him the friend he professed to be.

Simon's tie was a mess. He pulled it loose and started over.

"He's not that good looking," he grumbled.

Who was he kidding? Trevor was a god. Adonis dressed in Armani.

"I don't want to see her get hurt," he told his reflection.

And he was worried that she would despite her assurances that she had no real interest in Trevor beyond thinking he was hot and wanting him to take her to the reunion so that the other women there, especially a certain three, would turn green with envy. He pictured Chloe and Trevor walking into the old gym, the guy's hands resting in places that, while respectable, still held an overtone of intimacy. They'd share a dance. A laugh. Maybe steal a kiss or two. Chloe would get that dreamy look on her face and the other women would sigh, imagining the hot sex to come.

When he mangled the knot a second time, he decided to give up. After tossing the tie aside, he unbuttoned his collar.

He sighed heavily. "This is going to be a very long night."

* * *

The bell rang just as he came out of the bedroom. His housekeeper went to answer it.

It was Chloe. She was wearing a damp trench coat and water dripped from the tip of her closed umbrella onto the foyer floor before Mrs. Benson took both it and the coat.

"It's raining buckets out there," Chloe said. "I thought I'd need a rowboat to get here."

Simon glanced at the rain-splattered windows. According to the forecast, the worst of the storm was supposed to have subsided by now, but it was showing no signs of letting up. Surely that was an omen of some sort. Whether good or bad, though, he didn't know.

"The party doesn't start for another hour," he reminded her.

"I know, but I thought I'd come early." She pointed to her hair. "I straightened it for the occasion. Can you tell?"

It was a mess of corkscrews. In other words, adorable. He loved it this way, but he knew better than to say so. He knew better than to say *anything*. So, he kept his expression neutral and offered nothing more than a grunt that could be interpreted a number of different ways.

"I brought my flat iron, just in case." She'd brought more than that judging from the small suitcase she'd wheeled in behind her.

"You know, you could have gotten ready here and saved yourself the hassle of doing your hair twice."

"Next time."

Two words that caused an inappropriate amount of interest to lick up his spine like flames. To douse them, he crossed to the makeshift bar that had been set up in the corner and helped himself to a gin and tonic.

Chloe joined him there. "What do you think of my outfit?"

He took a liberal swig of his drink. She'd gone for understated with a copper-colored, cotton dress that she'd paired with wedge sandals. She wasn't limping… yet. In fact, given the graceful way she'd just crossed the room, he'd say the hours she'd been spending walking around her apartment in high heels with a book on her head were paying off. He focused on her toenails. They were painted a hue similar to that of the dress.

His gaze traveled back up her legs and stopped at the hem. Just what did she wear with her heels when she walked around her apartment with that book on her head? A dress such as this one? Or maybe shorts and a T-shirt. Or…or…

"I'm a dead man."

"What?"

He coughed. "That dress. It's killer. Hence my…um deadness." He coughed again.

Chloe frowned. "Are you all right? You're not coming down with something I hope."

He nearly laughed at that. Coming down with something? Hardly. He had a full-blown case and he'd probably suffer from it for the rest of his life.

"I'm fine." He gave his chest a couple of thumps. "My

drink went down the wrong pipe is all. Getting back to your outfit, is it new?"

"Sort of."

"How can something be sort of new?"

"I went to a secondhand shop in the Village that my sister told me about. It carries mostly designer label stuff, castoffs from the well-to-do." She plucked at the fabric and grinned in triumph. "This retailed for three times what I paid for it."

"Is it another contender for the reunion?"

"No, but I felt it an essential investment in my pre-reunion preparations."

"Like the whitened teeth."

"Exactly. As for the reunion, I've decided to go with black."

"The color of mourning." He sipped his drink again.

"It's also a power color. And classic for formal occasions," she replied primly.

"The reunion is in the old high school gym. How formal will it be? I'm thinking of wearing my workout clothes."

"You are not."

He shrugged. "Fine, but I'm not wearing a tux."

"But you'll put on a suit, right?"

"I'm thinking sport coat and maybe no tie. Kind of like what I'm wearing tonight." He pushed away thoughts of the mangled length of silk he'd tossed in his closet.

Chloe was frowning. "Do you think Trevor will wear a suit?"

Already she was banking on the man as her date. Simon's grip tightened on the tumbler in his hand.

"I'm not a mind reader. You'll have to ask him." The words came out harsh, so he moderated his tone and changed the subject. "Getting back to your dress, non-power-color that it is, you still look amazing."

She smiled shyly and her gaze slid to the side. Just as she had the other night, she didn't try to brush off the compliment.

"That looks good on you."

"What?" She looked confused.

"Confidence."

She eyed him a moment, obviously searching for a response. He figured she couldn't find one, because what she said was, "Do you mind if I use the bathroom in your room to revisit my hair? More room to spread out my stuff."

He glanced at the suitcase again. "Not at all."

"Thanks. It won't take me long. When I'm done, I can help you set up."

"Don't worry. I have a staff for that," he said. "And I hired some extra people to help out this evening."

The added help arrived about the time Chloe began obliterating her curls with a flat iron, and included a caterer, a bartender and some waitstaff to see to his guests' needs. Simon needed the extra hands now that his small soiree had ballooned to more than three dozen people.

He blamed Chloe for that. He'd tried to keep it small, no more than a handful of guests, but she'd insisted that if it were too intimate a gathering, Trevor might suspect a setup.

When Trevor arrived fashionably late more than an hour into the party, it became clear he'd been none the wiser. He brought a date, a lithe and leggy young woman who dwarfed every female in the room and quite a few of the men. Including Trevor. She even had an inch or two on Simon. And she was wearing flats.

"Who is the Amazon?" Chloe wanted to know.

"No idea."

Chloe crossed her arms over her chest and tapped her nearly empty glass of white wine against one biceps. "God, this is just great. Did you know he was seeing someone?"

"He's *always* seeing someone, Chloe. I told you that. The guy is a serial dater."

"Like you?" she asked with a subtle arch of one brow.

Since he couldn't argue the accuracy of her assessment, he didn't try, but he pointed out their differences. "Worse. He moves on to his next victim before he's finished with his current one."

"Yeah, she looks like a victim," Chloe muttered. "All six-plus feet of her."

"She's crying on the inside. She just doesn't know it yet," Simon said, earning a half-hearted chuckle.

Chloe's laughter stopped abruptly. "Oh, my God! They're coming this way."

"Of course they are. I'm the host."

"And I'm out of here."

"Too late." He put a hand on her arm. "Stay. Face them." When she continued to edge away, Simon pulled out his trump card. "Consider it good practice for the reunion."

He wasn't sure whether to laugh or groan when Chloe squared her shoulders and her face brightened with a smile.

"Simon, great party," Trevor said. The two men clasped hands.

"Glad you could make it."

"Yeah. Sorry we're late."

"The weather is horrible," Chloe commiserated.

Trevor nodded, but his smile turned carnal when he added, "We decided to wait out the worst of it in my apartment."

The Amazon issued a smoky laugh that could have served as foreplay.

"This is Shauna Ferrone," Trevor was saying. "Shauna, this is Simon Ford and, I'm sorry, I can't quite remember your name."

Ouch. Simon nearly winced on Chloe's behalf, though part of him was overjoyed that his oversexed colleague apparently hadn't catalogued her in his mental black book.

"Chloe McDaniels."

"Chloe. Right. Simon's friend." Trevor nodded, his expression turning speculative again as his gaze traveled south.

His date seemed to notice. "My Pomapoo is named Chloe," she said.

"Pomapoo?" Simon asked.

"She's half Pomeranian and half toy poodle."

One of those trendy little designer dogs for which an entire industry of clothing and accessories had been born. Next to him, Chloe was poised like a pit bull ready to attack.

"It's nice to meet you, Shauna. So, are you a lawyer like Trevor?" he asked.

The woman looked insulted. "You don't know who I am?"

"I'm...afraid not." Simon glanced at Chloe for support. She gave an imperceptible lift of her shoulders.

"I design jewelry," the woman said. "Celebrities clamor to wear my pieces on the red carpet."

"Shauna crafted the necklace the first lady wore at the inaugural ball," Trevor supplied. Simon doubted he cared in the least who the woman had designed jewelry for, but Trevor was a man hoping to get lucky, so he had to look suitably impressed.

"I can't believe you didn't know that, Simon." This from Chloe, whose eyes shimmered with amusement. To Shauna, she said, "You'll have to forgive him. You know how men can be. They don't pay attention to such things."

Shauna tossed her mane of perfect waves. She was a beautiful woman, if self-centered. Standing next to her, Chloe looked simple, but in the best possible way. Even wearing more makeup than normal and dressed über-fashionably she exuded an authenticity that the Shaunas of the world couldn't match.

"Is this piece one of yours?" Chloe pointed to the gemstone necklace that fell into Shauna's décolletage.

"Yes. It's one of my favorites."

"I can see why. Can I get you a drink?" she asked, steering the woman toward the bar.

That was Chloe. She might not like someone, but she would always be polite and find common ground for conversation. She was so easy to talk to.

"I can't believe your friend's name slipped my mind," Trevor said. "I hope I didn't offend her."

"She'll get over it."

"Is she…seeing anyone?"

Simon's hand froze halfway to bringing his drink to his mouth. Here was the moment Chloe was hoping for.

"No. She's not seeing anyone." Only, that wasn't what made it past Simon's lips. Rather, he said, "Yeah. She's involved."

"Oh. Is it serious?"

Take a hint, dude, he wanted to say. Instead, he nodded. "I think so. Maybe even heading-to-the-altar serious."

"Really." Trevor rocked back on his heels. "I got a totally different vibe from her the other day in your office."

"Cold feet." He shrugged. "She told me tonight she's pretty sure he's about to pop the question."

Trevor glanced around. "Is he here?"

"No. He's…away on business. He travels a lot. He's a…a…an archaeologist." Simon was astounded at the lies popping out of his mouth. And ashamed, of course. Really ashamed.

"No kidding."

Ashamed or not, they just kept coming. "Seriously. He digs up dinosaur fossils and…and stuff like that for a living. He's on a big dig now. It could change the theory of evolution."

Trevor looked impressed. Hell, Simon was impressed. But then, no one was too good for Chloe.

Neanderthal that Trevor was, he honed in on only one detail. "So, he's gone a lot?"

Uh-oh. "Yeah. But he'll be cutting back on travel soon. You know, with their wedding right around the corner."

"Too bad. She looks like she'd be a lot of fun," Trevor said.

Fun. That was code for a good romp, in Trevor-speak. Simon gritted his teeth. No doubt Trevor was already considering offering to be a last fling.

"Yeah. Chloe's really great. Smart, funny." He sipped his drink. "She has a black belt in jujitsu, you know."

"Jujitsu?"

Simon made a chopping motion with his hand. "She could probably kick your ass."

Trevor frowned. Simon held back a smile. Judging from the women his colleague had dated, it was clear he preferred strong females, but probably not the kind who could flip him over one shoulder and then crush his larynx with their bare hands.

"Is that how she keeps in shape?"

Great, now he was checking out her body. What was with this guy?

"Nah. Weight lifting. She can bench press almost as much as I can. It might not be obvious now, but she considered going into professional body building at one time."

Trevor grimaced. "Those chicks are scary. Arnold Schwarzenegger in a bikini." It was exactly what Simon wanted to hear. Until the other man added, "I'm glad she changed her mind. She's not all grossly sinewy now and she has a really nice...upper body."

"They're fake."

"How do you...?" Trevor's eyes narrowed. "Have you guys ever dated?"

"Me and Chloe?" He laughed. Maybe a little too loudly and a little too long. He reeled in his manufactured mirth. "Nah. We're just friends."

Trevor's eyebrows bobbed. Like the rest of the man, they were a little too perfect. Simon suspected waxing. "Friends with benefits?"

Simon wanted to punch him. One solid jab to that Brad Pitt-like jaw.

"It's not like that. Chloe and I have known one another since we were kids." Across the room, he saw her laugh at something Shauna said. She was a good listener. Even when she was bored, she always gave the appearance of hanging on the speaker's every word. As he watched, she reached up to push a straightened bunch of hair behind one ear. A flash of silver caught his eye. The small hoop earrings had been a gift from him for her twenty-first birthday. All these years later, she still wore them, even though they weren't especially flashy or expensive. He hadn't been able to afford expensive back then. "She's like my sister."

Trevor's laughter could be heard over the music and conversation. "Just a heads up, friend. Society frowns on guys looking at their sisters the way you're looking at Chloe right now."

"I'm not looking—"

Trevor cut him off. "It must really suck that she's seeing someone else."

No, what sucked was that she didn't *see* Simon.

Not that he wanted her to, he amended quickly. That unspoken lie, unlike the whoppers he'd just told Trevor, left a nasty taste in his mouth.

"Want a drink?" God knew Simon could use a refill.

"Sure."

It was closing in on two in the morning. The party was on its last leg and so was Simon. Most of the guests already had left, including Trevor and Shauna. In fact, they were among the first to leave. With the food nearly gone and the bar running low, the last of the holdouts finally staggered toward the exit and the cabs Simon had called to ferry them home.

He'd dismissed his housekeeper early in the evening and then the waitstaff and bartender just before one o'clock. He'd seen no need for them to hang around for the handful of his colleagues who'd remained. Now, finally, he was alone.

Except for Chloe.

He found her in the kitchen, standing next to a platter of cold *hors d'oeuvres* and staring at them with a covetous expression.

"Step away from the stuffed mushrooms," he commanded in an appropriately stern voice.

She actually jumped.

"I've only had one. Okay, two, but I dropped half of the second one on the floor, so it doesn't count."

"How much have you had to drink?" He'd counted at least three glasses of wine, but then he hadn't been with her every moment of the evening. She could have slipped in a fourth. Maybe even a fifth.

"Not nearly enough." She sighed and levered herself up onto the granite countertop. One wedge sandal hit the floor, followed by the other. She wiggled her toes and sighed again.

"I'm sorry the night didn't turn out how you'd hoped."

Guilt nipped at him after he said it, since Trevor had expressed interest in her and might very well have approached her if not for Simon's comments. He shouldn't have lied and said she was involved with someone. As for the jujitsu and power-lifting comments, they weren't completely baseless. She'd taken an aerobic kickboxing class last summer, and when they went for their morning jogs, she often carried hand weights.

"He asked me out."

"Wh-wh-what?" he sputtered. "Who?"

"Trevor."

That son of a… "Even after I…"

"Even after you what?"

"Nothing." He popped a cold stuffed mushroom into his mouth, stalling as he searched for a plausible response. It turned out he didn't need one.

"You were right about him, Simon. He's a serial dater of the worst sort. Here he is out with a beautiful and interesting—if totally self-absorbed—woman, and the moment she excuses herself to go to the restroom, he comes on to me. Me!" She frowned. "For some reason, he asked me to show him some martial arts moves."

Simon swallowed. "Kinky."

"A guy like that is a snake, no matter how gorgeous."

"So, you said no?"

"I'll probably regret this for the rest of my life, but yes. I said no. My luck, if he'd gone with me to the reunion he would have hit on my archrival."

Whatever the reason, Simon wasn't going to quibble. "I'm glad."

"Yeah, and I'm dateless for the reunion." She fussed with her hair, pulling it into a ponytail at the back of her head before letting it fall free. It spread around her shoulders in a fiery cascade. He jerked his gaze away before a full-fledged fantasy could form and focused on her bare feet instead.

"You kept your shoes on until the guests left. That's a record."

She smiled and stretched out her legs. Copper-tipped toes wiggled again. He swallowed. Damn those fantasies. They just kept coming.

"I'm paying for it now," she was saying.

"Here, let me." It was pure folly and he would regret it later. But he pulled a chair in front of her and sat down. Taking one slender foot in his hands, he began to massage the arch. Her eyelids slid shut and her expression turned rhapsodic. The moan that escaped was nearly his undoing.

"You've got great hands," she said.

"This isn't even my best work."

Her eyes opened. Neither of them said anything as the moment stretched. All the while, he continued his ministrations on her instep.

"Don't...don't neglect the other one," she whispered when his hands finally stilled.

He did as instructed.

"You've got such soft skin." He was no longer rubbing her foot. He'd worked his way up to her calf. "It feels like silk."

"I...I...always apply lotion right after I get out of the shower," she told him. Simon didn't think he'd ever heard her sound quite so breathless. Unless it was after a run. "It locks in mmm-moisture."

"I'll have to remember that." It was his voice that sounded breathless now. He started to work on the other leg from ankle to knee. "Do you...apply it all over?"

"On every inch of me."

"That must take a while."

"Uh-huh. If you do it right." The knuckles on the hands wrapped around the edge of the countertop turned white, telling Simon that he was doing something right.

"Anything worth doing is worth doing right."

He rose from his chair. His hands caressed the backs of her knees, finding a sensitive spot that caused her to moan. He knew he should stop. He was flirting with disaster. He never should have let it get this far. He wanted to blame his lapse in control on the beverages he'd consumed. But he'd cut himself off over two hours earlier, and even then after only three relatively diluted gin and tonics. No, what had him intoxicated now was the woman before him. The woman whose legs he was literally standing between.

"I…I must have had more to drink than I thought," Chloe said. She pulled her legs free, swiveled to the side and hopped down.

So, she was going to use the excuse he'd already discarded. He would let her.

"Light-headed?"

"Out of my mind," it sounded like she muttered. Or maybe he just needed her to say something to that effect. He didn't want to be the only one who felt so desperate and disturbed.

"Maybe you should stay here. I hate the thought of you going home at this hour, especially if you're a little drunk."

"I'm not drunk."

"You just said—"

"Light-headed. Which could be attributed to not eating more than a few appetizers all evening."

"I've got leftover pizza in the fridge. It's from our favorite place."

"At this time of night? Too many calories and fat grams. That kind of indulgence requires a strenuous workout afterward to keep the guilt at bay."

"I can think of a strenuous workout."

She blinked at that, but was the color rising in her cheeks from surprise or interest? He decided not to find out. Too much was at stake to change the rules of their relationship now. "We're going running in the morning, aren't we?"

Chloe nodded vigorously. "Of course. Exactly. I knew that was what you meant."

"Does that mean you'll have some pizza?"

"It means you'd better call me a cab before I make a huge mistake."

He nodded. He knew exactly what she meant.

CHAPTER TEN

Best Complexion

PANIC BUILT AS the taxi Chloe had splurged on crawled through midday Manhattan traffic.

What was she going to do?

Well, besides lock herself in her apartment and live like a hermit until several layers of her epidermis had sloughed off.

How come she had to get the one person at the tanning salon who was new and, well, stupid? These kinds of mistakes had a way of finding Chloe. It was as if she'd been born as the test subject for practical jokes and laughable mishaps.

Only, she wasn't laughing.

She was hiding.

And probably looking like a wannabe celebrity with a scarf pulled over her hair and a pair of oversized sunglasses covering much of her face. She'd bought both from a street vendor outside the salon who'd been so preoccupied with her appearance that he hadn't even bothered to try to sell her any of the knockoff designer watches strapped to his arms.

The cabdriver was eyeing her in the rearview mirror. Since she was talking to herself, she understood why.

"It's going to be okay. It's going to be okay." She'd been chanting those words since leaving the salon.

"I've changed my mind," she said. When the driver didn't respond, she leaned forward and tapped the Plexiglas partition. "I've changed my mind."

"It's not going to be okay?" he asked warily.

Chloe cleared her throat. "No. I mean, yes. It's going to be…forget it. I've changed my mind about where I want you to take me."

She rattled off a new address and leaned back in her seat, where she continued her chant. Fifteen minutes later, the taxi driver pulled his cab to a stop outside Ford Technology Solutions, where Chloe quickly dashed inside, slipped into the first available elevator and rudely closed the door on the man rushing toward it, calling, "Hold, please!"

It was lunchtime, so Simon's secretary wasn't manning her usual guard post outside his office. But he was there. He'd mentioned during an earlier phone conversation that he was going to eat a sandwich at his desk while preparing for an afternoon meeting. She nearly went limp with relief when she spied him. Lunch and a sheaf of papers were spread out in front of him. His tie was askew, his shirtsleeves rolled nearly to his elbows. His thick and usually neatly combed hair was mussed, probably from running his fingers through it. She liked it better this way. She found it sexy.

More and more lately, Chloe was finding things about Simon to be sexy. The way he'd rubbed her feet the other night definitely qualified. She'd engaged in foreplay that hadn't left her that breathless and keyed up.

A warning bell went off in her head. She'd done her damnedest not to recall that night or her reaction. She concentrated on the attributes that had brought her here today. Simon was dependable, level-headed and pragmatic. He would know what to do.

Apparently that was to choke on a mouthful of smoked turkey on whole wheat and spill his opened bottle of water on his desktop.

"Chloe?" He thumped his chest and reached for a napkin to blot the soggy papers. "I can't believe you got past security wearing that outfit. Are you impersonating a celebrity or something?"

"Something," she replied on a sigh and pulled off the sunglasses and scarf.

His eyes widened. "Good God! You're—"

"Don't say it," she warned. Actually, the words came out more as a plea.

But Simon apparently couldn't stop himself from stating the obvious: "You're orange."

She wanted to cry. In fact, she already had cried in the salon's changing room. The only thing a good bout of tears had accomplished, however, was to make her eyes puffy and red-rimmed. Now they clashed with her new complexion.

Simon tossed the wet napkins into the trash. "Actually, you're more tangerine than orange."

She nodded, as if the distinction made a bit of difference. The fact remained that Chloe looked as if she had escaped from a box of crayons.

"Mind telling me what happened?"

"I went to a tanning salon. Frannie suggested—"

"Why do you listen to her?"

She ignored him and went on. "Frannie suggested I get a faux tan and gave me the name of the place where she goes. Well, they were busy today. One of the sprayer thingies was broken, and someone had called in sick. The girl who'd just been hired last week to staff the reception desk was pitching in." Chloe worked up a smile. No doubt her whitened teeth gleamed against her new skin tone. "On the bright side, I didn't have to pay for my session."

"I should hope not."

Her bottom lip wobbled. "Is it as bad as I think?"

"No. Uh-uh." The fierce way he shook his head was overkill. "The, um, lighting in here is horrible. It gives everything an orange, er, tangerine tint."

He was lying and badly, but she loved him for it. She collapsed into one of the chairs that faced his desk.

"All I wanted was a nice glow, something to tone down my fish-belly whiteness."

"Your skin color is called alabaster."

"I was just going for off-white," she cried. "I wanted to camouflage my freckles."

"I like your freckles."

She scrunched her eyes closed. "My freckles are the least of my problems now."

"So, exactly what happened?"

"I got a teeny-bopper named Cinnamon—"

"Cinnamon? Are you kidding? Her parents actually named her after a spice?"

"It happens. Think Rosemary or Sage."

Simon nodded in consideration. "Now that you mention it, I went to college with a guy called Basil, and my cousin named her first-born Dill." He shook his head. "Scratch that. I think his full name is Dillon."

Chloe snapped her fingers. "Can I get back to my story, please?"

"Sure. Sorry." He picked up his sandwich and motioned for her to continue.

"So, this Cinnamon girl apparently failed the remedial reading class at her school and…" Chloe's words trailed off and she let her head fall back on an exasperated shriek. Studying the ceiling tiles, she asked, "Why do the cosmos hate me?"

Simon didn't bother trying to answer the unanswerable. He was too practical for that, which was precisely why she'd hightailed it to his office when any sane person would have gone home and begun scrubbing with a loofah.

"It's a fake tan, right?"

A grunt served as her reply.

"It will fade long before the reunion, which isn't for three weeks."

"Two weeks and four days." But she straightened in her chair.

"That's plenty of time."

Chloe sniffled. "Do you really think so?"

"I know so. You'll be back to alabaster in no time."

"Alabaster. You know, that does have a better ring to it than fish-belly white," she conceded.

"You have lovely skin, Chloe. And, as I discovered the other night, incredibly soft."

Her hands stilled. Her pulse, meanwhile, took off like a thoroughbred coming out of the chute on race day. She'd replayed every second of their encounter in his kitchen a dozen times since then, wondering what might have happened if she'd stayed. Wishing...

She realized she was staring at him. He was staring at her, too, his expression indecipherable, which was odd. She'd known him so long that she felt she could read him like a book. Well, if he were a book now, he was written in hieroglyphics.

"What are you thinking, Simon?"

Why had she asked him that? Not that she wasn't curious, but she was in the middle of a crisis and... and...and there had to be some other reason the topic was off-limits.

"What am I thinking?"

Here was her opportunity to back away. But did she take it? "What's on your mind?"

He put down what remained of his sandwich and wiped his hands on a napkin. "The same thing that's been on my mind for quite a while."

Oh, that was helpful. He could be referring to baseball or work or—and she'd kill him for this—that hot new girl at the lobby's reception desk that Chloe had spied on her mad dash to the elevators.

Let it go, she told herself. She asked, "Does it have anything to do with…me?"

God! She wanted to slap a hand over her mouth, maybe follow it up with several layers of duct tape. The question hung in the air between them. His expression remained unreadable.

Finally, he said, "It does."

Two simple words and her breath hitched. It actually *hitched*.

Chloe tried to remember another time in the company of another man when her breath had caught in her throat before shuddering out. The best she could come up with was Justin Timberlake back when he was part of *NSYNC and she'd saved up her allowance for a whole month to buy a ticket to the group's upcoming concert. For weeks beforehand, she'd listened to the band's latest CD, singing into her hairbrush and dancing in front of the mirror in her bedroom, all the while dreaming of catching Justin's eye at the upcoming concert.

She hadn't. No big surprise there since her seat had been about three miles from the stage.

Other than that, even the men she'd dated post-college, the very ones she'd claimed had stomped all over her heart and prompted her to overindulge in ice cream, had never caused her respiratory tract to go all wonky like this.

"H-h-how?"

He expelled a breath and then said her name.

Suddenly, she didn't want to know. She was misreading signals and being foolish. If Simon were interested in her that way, he would have said something. As it was, since he hadn't, she'd been content with his friendship. Well, maybe not completely content, but she'd accepted it since she didn't want to lose him.

"Getting back to my situation, I guess I can be thankful I went for a trial run."

His brow crinkled.

"At the tanning salon," she clarified. "Can you imagine if the reunion were this weekend?"

She wasn't acting when she shuddered.

"Would you have gone?" he asked.

"What? And give those girls another reason to tease me? Not a chance. It's bad enough I'll be showing up dateless."

"You could go with me, you know."

He was being practical. After all, he and Chloe would wind up sitting together anyway. Just as whoever they brought with them would wind up being bored.

"Aren't you bringing a date?"

He shrugged. "I'm not seeing anyone."

But he could find a date if he wanted. Someone totally hot and drool-worthy. Simon had long ago outgrown his geekiness. Well, what other people considered geekiness. Add in a successful career and a touch of standoffishness that women couldn't resist, and members of the opposite sex were all but lined up outside his door.

Chloe swallowed. "It's all right, you know."

"What's all right?"

"You don't have to take pity on me. Bring someone to the reunion if you'd like." She nodded and worked up a smile, hoping to seem more convincing. "That model you dated awhile ago would probably go with you. You parted on good terms. If you bring her, every guy in the place would drool."

"That's the thing, Chloe, I don't see the need to make them drool."

She tilted her head. "You don't harbor just a little resentment toward them for the way they treated you?"

"If I did, it's long over. They didn't like me because they didn't understand me. I was…weird."

"You were not."

"Mature, then."

"I'll give you that," she agreed.

"Whatever. It was a long time ago. I turned out okay."

Chloe laughed. "That's a total understatement and we both know it. You're company will make the Fortune 500 within the next couple of years."

"Assuming we continue the current level of growth," he added, matter-of-fact. No braggadocio was required when you had the business community's respect to back it up.

"Have I ever told you how proud I am of you?"

He glanced away. "A time or twelve."

"That's because I am. You are amazing, Simon. Not just because you're smart and a whiz at what you do professionally. But because even when you're supposed to be going over notes for a meeting, you make time for a friend who's in the midst of a crisis."

"You're orange," he said deadpan. "What was I supposed to do?"

She laughed. "This is exactly what I'm talking about. You can make me see the humor in this."

"You would have eventually."

"Eventually," she agreed. Ten or twenty years from now, she probably would laugh like a loon. "But thanks for helping me see it now."

"You're amazing, too, you know. I'm proud of you, Chloe."

"But I haven't—"

"Haven't what?" he demanded almost angrily. "You graduated with honors from high school despite constant bullying and an older sister who was only too happy to keep you in her shadow. You graduated from college in four years, paying for a good chunk of it yourself."

"You did the same."

"I had a full-ride scholarship."

"Because you're so stinking smart."

He rose abruptly to his feet. "Don't do that."

"What?"

"I'm sick of you taking shots at yourself. It's bad enough you had to endure them from Natasha and company during high school. And your sister certainly doesn't help your self-esteem."

"Frannie?"

"She's jealous of you. Always has been. Always will be."

She gaped at him and said again, "Frannie?"

Simon waved a hand. "I'm not going to sit here and listen to you denigrate yourself."

"Actually, you're standing."

"I'm…" He put his hands on his waist. His tone was impatient when he asked, "Is that all you're taking away from this conversation?"

Chloe blinked. "I…don't know."

"Then, let me clarify it for you." He stalked around the desk, grabbed her by the arms and hauled her to her feet. "You're a good person, Chloe. You're kind and funny and plenty smart. You're also beautiful and…and as sexy as hell!"

"You're yelling."

"Yes, I'm yelling. Because I'm mad."

"Why?"

"Because you keep settling for less. You settle for idiots who say the right things but never follow through on the promises they make. You settle for a part-time position because your boss claims that's all that is available when you have the skills and credentials to go elsewhere."

"Mr. Thompson—"

"Is taking gross advantage of you. Again, because you let him. You're a doormat. For your boss, for your sister, for the men you date. For that matter, when are you going to stop letting a bunch of jealous and insecure girls you haven't seen in a decade dictate your life?"

"They're not dictating my life."

He snorted. "Chloe, you're contorting yourself to fit their idea of perfect."

"I wouldn't say that."

"You're orange! Orange!"

"We agreed on tangerine. And it was a mistake on the salon's part."

"The only mistake was that you were at the salon— Frannie's suggestion, by the way—in the first place."

"What do you want from me, Simon?"

"I want…I want…" The hands gripping her shoulders tightened before dropping away. "I just want you to be happy. I want you to look in the mirror and be pleased with the woman who's looking back at you."

"I like myself."

"I want you to love yourself."

"I do."

"Do you?"

"Of course. Well, most of the time. I'm not perfect, but I'm getting there."

"See, I don't agree. I think you've been perfect all along."

"That's because you're my friend." The words were automatic. His scowl told her how off the mark he found them. Once again, her breath hitched.

"Your friend." He scrubbed a hand over his jaw and glanced away.

"Sim—"

He hauled her into his arms. Her breath and the rest of his name whooshed out when she came into contact with the solid expanse of his chest. His face was so close to hers that she could see the flecks of gold in his brown eyes. Odd, she'd never noticed the intricacies of his eye color. Before she could comment on it, his mouth lowered to hers.

Chloe told herself it was surprise that kept her from pulling back. Just as it was surprise that had her opening her lips and granting him access. Good heavens, the man could kiss even better than she'd been expecting. And, oh yeah, she could admit she'd been anticipating this moment. Eager for it in the way one is eager for the plunge before cresting the highest peak of a roller coaster.

"Friends don't kiss like this." The words followed her ragged sigh when the kiss ended.

His eyes were pinched closed. "I know. Should I apologize?"

"No, but…"

"But?"

"I don't know."

He blew out a breath and nodded. "Well, I do know."

"What?"

"I need to apologize. I was trying to get you to see yourself through a pair of objective eyes. I went too far."

"So the kiss…" She swallowed around the lump that had formed in her throat. "It was like a life lesson?"

Say no. Say no. Say no.

Simon had always seemed able to read her mind in the past. Now, it was painfully clear he was not telepathic. "Yes. I'm sorry. It was wrong of me."

"I…well…" She settled a hand on one hip. Between

that damned lump and confusion, she wasn't sure what to say.

"Mr. Ford… Oh, Chloe." His secretary glanced between the two of them. Whatever she thought of the situation—or Chloe's orange skin tone—she was too professional to let it show. "Those other charts you wanted were faxed over while I was at lunch."

Simon backed away, nodded. "Terrific. Great. I'll have a look at them now."

"I was just leaving," Chloe said.

His secretary withdrew.

"Chloe, you…"

"I have to go." She pulled the scarf back into place and plopped the glasses on the bridge of her nose. "Sorry to have bothered you."

"You know better than that."

She didn't know anything at the moment, except that if she stayed much longer, she was going to cry.

She backed out the door, nodded. "And thanks."

"For…?"

Good thing for the dark glasses. Despite her best efforts, her eyes were filling. "The life lesson."

It wasn't one she would soon forget.

Simon had screwed up royally.

He knew that even before he watched Chloe dash away. Sunglasses or not, she'd been on the verge of crying.

Go after her, he told himself. Apologize and explain. But he returned to the chair behind his desk instead. An apology was what had caused her hurt feelings.

Another one would only make matters worse. As for an explanation, he didn't have one. Not one she would understand.

"I love you" weren't words he used often or, when it came to women, ever. But he knew without a doubt that he loved Chloe. He'd always loved her.

The only thing more painful than being in love with her was hurting her.

And now he'd done just that.

CHAPTER ELEVEN

Most Focused

CHLOE COULDN'T THINK straight.

She soaked in the tub, catching the drips from the leaky faucet with the tip of one prunelike toe and trying to wrap her mind around what had happened.

And she wasn't talking about her skin tone, even though this was her third bath in two hours. The first two had been as hot as she could stand. She'd gone through an entire bottle of body scrub and two loofah sponges. She couldn't tell if her skin was less orange since it was now red and irritated. Which is why she'd opted for a third bath. This one had started out tepid and had since grown cold. She was too preoccupied to care.

Simon had kissed her. He had *really* kissed her. With passion and purpose and, for a moment she'd thought, promise. The earth had moved. Maybe that was being a bit dramatic, but Chloe definitely had felt off-kilter afterward.

And ridiculously hopeful until he'd apologized

and chalked it up to a life lesson. She hadn't seen that coming.

She would be the first to admit that she wasn't good at reading men. She had a hard time assessing their true feelings and their level of interest in her—well, beyond sex. It had led to a lot of heartache over the years, as well as one particularly embarrassing situation involving a guy from her political-science class who had flirted outrageously with her. On Frannie's advice, Chloe had gone to his dorm room after finals armed with a bottle of wine and a box of pizza. (It was college and pizza was all she could afford, especially since she'd splurged on the wine. No twist-off cap this time. Nope. She'd gone for a bottle with a bona fide cork.)

She'd felt like one of the cast from *Sex and the City* until a beautiful young woman answered the door. Mortified to discover that Mr. Flirtatious was all but engaged, she'd handed over the wine and pizza, and pretended to have been paid to deliver both. The night wasn't a total bust. She'd made back five bucks in a tip. But it was yet more proof of her ineptness when it came to reading men.

Still, she'd always thought she understood Simon. He said what he meant. He was up front. No subterfuge. No game playing. Straightforward.

Until lately.

Right now, thanks to that amazing kiss, Chloe found him to be a full-blown enigma.

A life lesson? Seriously? He'd kissed her in his office to *teach* her something? That wasn't like him. Oh, Simon had given her plenty of advice and instruction over the years, but it had been constructive and helpful. It had never caused her to question…everything.

The phone rang. By the time Chloe toweled off and pulled on a robe, the call had already gone to voice mail. It was her sister. Frannie had heard from a friend about what happened at the tanning salon and was calling to see if there was anything she could do.

Chloe dialed Frannie's number and waited for her sister to answer. Children's shrieks could be heard before a woman's weary-sounding hello made it through.

"Hey, it's me. Sorry I missed your call. I was in the tub when you called."

"Chloe, hey. Just a minute, okay?" Muffled threats followed. And then there was silence. Frannie's children had either obeyed her commands or had been bought off with cookies.

"I'm back. How are you? Or, I should ask, how is your skin? According to Melanie Lester, the people at the salon said you were all but glowing when you left."

"Did they?" And here they'd assured Chloe that the orange tint was barely noticeable.

"How did the bath work?" Frannie wanted to know. "Did some of it come off?"

Chloe studied the backs of her hands. "It's hard to say, since I'm red from all the scrubbing. I think I sloughed off several layers of skin."

On the other end of the line, Frannie sighed. "I'm sorry, Chloe. I know you wanted to look your absolute best for the reunion. On the bright side, your freckles won't be so noticeable now."

Simon was right, she realized. Her sister always did this. Whenever something bad or disappointing happened in Chloe's life, Frannie was the first to commiserate with her. There was nothing wrong with that, except that Frannie, who'd always been popular and pretty, never encouraged her younger sister to keep trying. Indeed, she often accepted defeat long before Chloe did. And sometimes had a hand in talking Chloe into accepting it, as well.

She recalled some of those incidents now.

In middle school:

Chloe, hon, you're just not cut out to be a cheerleader. You're too uncoordinated. But don't worry. You can always cheer from the stands with your friends.

In high school:

So what if you can't fit in the dress I wore to my prom? You need to accept that you'll always be a little chubby. We can't all be a size four or even a ten. Besides, you have pretty eyes.

And most recently:

If you were passed up for that promotion to full-time again, it's probably because Mr. Thompson doesn't think you're ready for it. Whatever you do, don't rock the boat. You'll find yourself out of a job. Do you know how hard it will be to find another one without a good recommendation from your former employer and an impressive resume?

Time and again, Frannie had encouraged her to

embrace the status quo, to settle for less, all the while implying that was all Chloe deserved.

"I'm not giving up," Chloe said now.

"What? What are you talking about?"

I'm talking about being happy. About being satisfied with myself and fulfilled in all aspects of my life.

"I'm talking about the reunion, of course. I'm going and I'll look spectacular. I've got some time yet. Nearly three weeks." Surely she would experience some more epidermal turnover by then. "Simon said it will fade."

"Simon? When did you see Simon?"

"I went to his office after leaving the salon."

"That was brave of you," Frannie murmured. "I would have hurried home and barricaded myself in my bedroom."

That had been Chloe's first inclination. She wondered now if she should have heeded it. Her life certainly wouldn't have been turned upside down.

"So, did Simon make you feel better?"

"He put things into perspective." Yep. They were clear as mud now.

"He's good at that."

Chloe frowned. "Frannie, what do you think of him?"

"Of Simon?" She sounded surprised and no wonder. It was like asking, what do you think of breathing? He was a constant in their lives. "What do you mean? As a man?"

"Yes." She hurried ahead with, "I'm thinking of fixing him up with a colleague from work. She's been in some bad relationships and she's, um, got a knack for picking some real losers."

"It sounds like the two of you should form a support group," Frannie remarked.

"Thanks." Between gritted teeth, Chloe said, "Could you just answer the question?"

"Simon's great. But you know that. The man is smart, good-looking and very successful. Given all of the women who have thrown themselves at him in recent years, I can't believe he's still single. For that matter, I'm a little surprised the two of you never... Forget it."

"Never what?"

"You know, got together. You get along better than most married couples. God knows, you're together as much as most married couples."

A ripple of excitement worked its way up Chloe's spine, but she forced herself to keep her sister's words in perspective. "We enjoy one another's company."

"Probably because you like the same weird things," Frannie said.

Chloe sniffed. "We have eclectic tastes."

"Weird. Eclectic. Same difference," Frannie said on a laugh. "You're the only two people I know who regularly flock to midnight showings of *The Rocky Horror Picture Show.*"

"It's a pop-culture phenomenon and your friends are boring."

"You know all of the songs by heart. You quote the lyrics in ordinary conversation. Time warps and what-not. People who aren't familiar with the movie probably think you're insane."

"I don't care what other people think." She frowned and realized that, when she was with Simon, having a good time, she really *didn't* care.

"And Sudoku puzzles," Frannie was saying.

"A lot of people like Sudoku puzzles. Where have you been? They're hugely popular and considered a good way to keep a person's mind sharp."

"Okay, but what about *Guess*. Honestly, who our age listens to *Guess?*"

"It's not *Guess*. It's *The Guess Who*. And we're not as much fans of the original group from the 1960s and '70s as we are of its former lead singer, especially the stuff he recorded after going solo." She hummed a few bars from "You Saved My Soul." "It's from 1981. Classic. And for the record, he's still around."

On the other end of the line, Frannie exhaled dramatically. "This is my point exactly. It's really too bad that you and Simon don't have any chemistry."

Chloe plucked at the lapels of her robe and felt her cheeks grow warm. If her face hadn't already been in the red-orange color family, it probably would be now. "Wh-what do you mean by that?"

"Well, for a while when you guys were in middle school and high school, I thought maybe Simon was interested in you. In fact, I thought Mom and Dad were nuts for letting him spend the night in your bedroom."

"He was upset and he slept on the floor."

"Still. He was a teenager. You were a teenager. Raging hormones and all. Kids nowadays hook up for kicks."

"You sound like Mom."

"That's because I'm *a* mom." She huffed. "My children aren't going to be left alone with members of the opposite sex until they're, like, thirty."

"Good luck with that."

Frannie ignored her and, unfortunately, got back to the subject that was making Chloe increasingly uncomfortable. "About you and Simon, every now and then when the two of you were in college, I thought I saw a glimmer of something pass between you. A look, a smile. But—" she sighed "—nothing ever came of it. Didn't you ever think about him in that way?"

"No! Never." A time or two. Maybe more. And too many times to count lately.

Frannie's laughter halted Chloe's musings. "Your long-term platonic relationship completely disproved my husband's theory, by the way."

Chloe was probably going to regret this, but she asked, "What's his theory?"

"That a man and a woman can't be just friends unless, well, either the guy is gay or the woman is really ugly."

"Simon's not gay!" Chloe shouted, incensed on his behalf. Then, incensed on her own, she added, "And I'm not ugly."

"Which is why it shot Matt's theory all to hell."

It was time to change the subject. She worked up a wounded tone, hoping to put Frannie on the offensive.

"You guys talk about me? Thanks. It's so nice to know my life is fodder for conversation in your home."

"We don't talk about you in a mean way," her sister soothed. But like a dog with a bone, Frannie wasn't letting go. "It's just that we do find it odd, Chloe. You date loser after loser and, in the meantime, you and Simon are both single and, well, the guy is hot."

Red alert! Red alert! Change the subject fast!

Unfortunately, Chloe's mouth ignored her brain's request. "You think Simon's hot?"

"You don't?"

"I…I…he kissed me," she blurted out. She reached for a throw pillow and whacked herself on the side of the head with it.

"Oh, my God! When did this happen?"

She decided to go with their most recent lip lock. "Today. In his office."

"Let me get this straight. You went to see him for reassurance after the salon fiasco and there you were, all neon orange and everything, and he…he *kissed* you?"

"That about sums it up. Yes."

"Describe the kiss."

Chloe held the phone away and pressed her face in the pillow so she could scream. To describe the kiss, she would have to think about it. And she'd been doing her damnedest not to.

"Chloe? Are you there?"

She lowered the pillow and returned the phone to her ear. "It was a kiss, Frannie. Surely, you've engaged in a few of those over the years."

Her sister wasn't dissuaded. "There are kisses and there are kisses." And wasn't *that* an understatement? "Describe it. In detail."

"He, um, came around his desk and…and he, um, pulled me in his arms."

"Where were his hands?"

Not where Chloe wanted them, she thought now. A moment ago, she'd been freezing. Now, she tossed off the throw and began fanning herself. "They were on my upper arms."

"Mmm. Sounds forceful. Like he meant business."

I think you've been perfect all along.

The words that had preceded the kiss echoed in Chloe's head now, throwing off her heart's steady rhythm.

"Did this kiss involve tongues?"

"God. I mean, what are we? Twelve?"

"I have two pre-schoolers and a husband whose idea of foreplay is to give them Popsicles and lock our bedroom door. Indulge me and answer the question."

It was the first inkling she had that her perfect sister's life wasn't as perfect as she'd always assumed.

"Fine. Yes. It involved tongues, Frannie," she said impatiently. "It was an adult-variety kiss."

"How was it?"

Friends don't kiss like that.

"It was…it was…"

Before she could finish, a crash sounded in the background, followed by a child's shrill scream. "How in the heck did you get up on the refrigerator?" Chloe heard

Frannie holler. Then, "I've got to go. I'll call you back after Matt gets home. I want to hear everything!"

She hung up even before Chloe could say goodbye.

Just after six that evening, the bell rang. All Chloe could see when she glanced through the peephole were flowers. Her heart did a funny flip and roll, only to drop into her stomach when she opened the door and found it was a deliveryman holding the bouquet.

The young man's eyes widened and he did a double-take. She could guess why. "Uh, Chloe McDaniels?"

"That's me."

"These are for you." He all but thrust the roses into her hands and then backed away. "Hope you're feeling better soon."

At least he hadn't said rest in peace, she decided as she closed the door. The roses were white and smelled as lush and gorgeous as they looked. The card tucked inside the blooms included two words and no signature. But she knew who'd sent them.

Forgive me?

Of course Chloe forgave Simon. She just needed to figure out for what. That was why she didn't call him that night. She didn't know what to say.

She was at work the next day when a second bouquet of flowers arrived. Another dozen, long-stem white roses bearing the same two-word question on the card. She couldn't continue to ignore Simon. So, she picked up the phone and dialed his office. His secretary put her through immediately.

"Hi. How are you?"

"Okay." How odd it was to feel tongue-tied and awkward around Simon.

"I'm glad you called. I was getting worried." He cleared his throat then. "Should I be worried?"

"No. But I am a little confused. What exactly do you want me to forgive you for?"

"I overstepped the bounds of our friendship."

"Uh-huh."

"And I lied to you."

"About?"

"It wasn't a damned life lesson. I mean, I wanted you to start seeing yourself as others see you, but that wasn't the reason I kissed you."

She pressed the receiver closer to her ear and wished for some privacy. Even a damned cubicle would be better than the open office she shared with three other graphic artists.

"Why did you?" she asked in a voice just above a whisper.

He was silent a moment. Then, "Can we just forget it ever happened?"

She wasn't sure whether to be insulted, hurt, relieved or mad. "That's not exactly an answer to my question."

"I don't want anything to change between us."

That wasn't really an answer, either, but she let it go. She had to since, when she glanced up, she spied Mr. Thompson making a beeline for her desk. "I've got to hang up."

"You're upset."

"Yes. Um, no. We'll talk another time, promise. But I can't right now. My boss is heading my way."

"Dinner tonight?" Simon pressed.

"Sorry. I'm working late. We have a big project that just came in requiring a quick turnaround."

"Please tell me you'll at least be getting paid over-time."

It was put a little more nicely than his earlier asser-tion that she was letting Mr. Thompson treat her as a doormat.

"I'm being a team player," she whispered into the phone. "Rumor has it there may be another full-time position opening up."

"That rumor always starts circulating when Mr. Thompson needs you to do him a favor."

He was right, of course. "I've gotta go." She slammed down the phone and beamed a grin at her portly boss. "I'm nearly done with the mock-up of that menu you wanted."

"Terrific." He nodded a moment before frowning. "Are you feeling okay, McDaniels? Your color is a little…off."

Chloe nearly laughed. *Off* was a compliment at this point after the rigorous scrubbings she'd endured during the past twenty-four hours. That morning, after another go at it with a loofah, she'd opted for long sleeves and pants despite the ninety-degree temperature outside. And she'd slathered a heavy layer of foundation over the raw skin of her face with the end result being a complexion that was more tomato than orange.

"I'm fine, Mr. Thompson. Just hard at work."

"Pace yourself. It's going to be a long day and an even longer evening."

"I thought you said we'd be out of here by seven?"

"That was before I remembered that my wife has a dinner party planned. I've got to leave by four. Stevens and Fournier," they were two of the other full-time graphic artists, "will be here until five."

"Five?" That was their normal quitting time.

"They have family obligations."

"That just leaves me and…" She glanced across her desk at the pasty-faced guy who'd beaten her out for the last full-time spot. "Gallagher."

"You can handle it. You're both hard workers."

The only difference being that, as a full-timer, Gallagher had better benefits and paid vacations.

"I don't know what I'd do without you, McDaniels."

"Offer me a full-time job and you may never have to find out."

She'd said the words so often in her head it took her a moment to realize she'd said them out loud. Instead of being mortified or unsettled, she felt empowered.

"You're such a kidder, McDaniels." He laughed so hard his jowls shook.

This was her chance. She could join in and pretend it had been a joke rather than a quasi-threat. *Doormat.* Or she could hold firm.

"Actually, I'm serious. You keep promising me full-time and telling me I've earned it."

"You have. You have. But no positions are available. I want to expand, but, right now, with the economy…" He lifted his shoulders. "You know how it is."

What she knew was that she was no longer willing to settle for the status quo. "But I've heard talk there would be a full-time position opening up if you sign this new account."

"I don't know how those crazy rumors start."

Simon's words came back to her. "I think I do."

"Hmm?"

"Nothing." She pushed her chair back from her desk and rose to her feet. "I can't stay, Mr. Thompson."

He blinked. "You can't…you have to!"

Across from her, Gallagher's pasty face turned a ghastly shade of green that almost made Chloe's tomato complexion attractive.

"I'm just a part-timer. I've already hit my quota of hours for the week."

"Fine. I'll pay you overtime."

His offer represented a victory. Oddly, it was no longer enough. "No."

She bent over to switch off her computer and then gathered up her purse.

"I'll give you a dollar an hour raise."

Another victory. Yet it too fell short. "Thanks. But no."

"You can't just walk out." He cleared his throat and his tone turned stern. "I'll fire you if you leave."

"There's no need for that."

"I'm glad you're seeing reason."

His smile was smug, making it all the easier for Chloe to inform him, "I quit."

CHAPTER TWELVE

Most Likely to Succeed

CHLOE DIDN'T HAVE much to take with her, which made clearing out her desk easy. One box of miscellaneous junk, a half-dead potted ivy and the flowers Simon had sent and she was ready to go. A sputtering Mr. Thompson followed her all the way downstairs to the door that led to the street.

"You're going to regret this," he warned.

"Perhaps. But I think I'd regret staying even more."

It was an exit made for Hollywood. She swore she heard music swell in the background as she turned and walked away with her head held high, her face aglow with as much dignity as manufactured melanin. When she reached the entrance for the subway, however, reality set in. As much as Chloe had wanted to pump her fists in the air like Rocky Balboa a few moments earlier, now she wanted to curl into a fetal position and begin sucking her thumb.

Oh, my God! What have I done?

She pulled out her cell phone. The first person she

thought to call was Simon. She went with Plan B and dialed Frannie instead. She knew it was a mistake even before her sister launched into lecture mode.

"You didn't!" Frannie didn't say it with "you go, girl!" admiration, either. Rather, her tone asked "Are you crazy?"

Chloe went on the defensive. "Mr. Thompson takes advantage of me on a regular basis. And I let him. Until today." She balanced the box on one hip and shifted the phone to her other ear as people streamed around her to go down the steps to the subway platform. "Well, I've had enough of it."

"Fine. Fine. Meanwhile, a few dozen other graphic designers will have their resumes on his desk by this time tomorrow, all of them eager to be *taken advantage of*."

Chloe pictured Frannie using her fingers to make annoying imaginary quote marks.

She was saying, "What are you going to do now? Hmm? How are you going to pay your bills?"

"The same way I was paying them before. Just barely."

"That's not funny."

"Nor is your appalling lack of support."

"Well, excuse me for being a realist." Frannie's sigh was both exaggerated and dramatic. "Mom and Dad are going to be so disappointed in you."

Chloe sucked in a deep breath and let it out slowly. Frannie always did this. Whenever she wanted Chloe to toe the line, she played the "parental disappointment card." Damn her. It always worked. Fear and a good dose of guilt already were making Chloe's stomach churn like a blender.

She fought back a wave of nausea.

"I'll have a job before they find out. Unless you tell them, that is."

"I won't lie to them."

"How is it lying when they don't know?"

"They're our parents." Frannie's tone turned self-righteous when she demanded, "Do you have any idea of the sacrifices they've made?"

What that had to do with Chloe quitting her job, she wasn't sure. It's not like she was planning to move back to Jersey and take up residence in her old bedroom. Her stomach did a slippery turn and roll anyway.

"I'll have a full-time job soon enough, one where I'm compensated appropriately for my skills and where my work ethic will be appreciated rather than exploited."

A passerby overheard her comment and gave Chloe a thumbs-up.

The theme from *Rocky* echoed in her head only to come to a screeching halt when her sister said, "That's a fine speech, Chloe. Tell it to your landlord when you can't scrape together the rent."

Suddenly, Chloe could picture herself back in her old bedroom, not only as a twenty-eight-year-old screw-up returning to the nest, but as a dried-up old spinster, the highlight of whose week was a new booklet of Sudoku puzzles.

"God, help me," she mumbled.

"What?"

Instead of replying, Chloe hung up. The move wasn't so much one of defiance as practicality. She was going to be sick.

On the bright side, she was eating light these days. On the not-so-bright side, she was standing on the street and the only thing to retch in was the box from her office. She was able to spare the bouquet of flowers. But both the box and the sorry-looking plant were dumped in the next garbage can Chloe found after she bypassed the subway entrance.

Instead of heading going home, she hailed a cab and gave the driver directions to Simon's apartment.

She needed him.

She told herself she was being foolish. She'd already told him that she would be working late. He probably was out with other friends for dinner or flying solo. Guys could do that without looking either desperate or pathetic. A woman seated alone in a restaurant? Whether or not it was the case, she might as well be holding a sign that read "I've been stood up."

Or he could be out with a woman. Worse, he could be *in* with one. The perky new receptionist from his office building came to mind. Chloe thought she might hurl again.

"I should call him."

"Did you say something, miss?" The cabdriver asked in a heavy Indian accent.

"No. Well, yes." She waved a hand. "But I'm talking to myself. I'm not crazy," she hastened to assure him. "I'm just...never mind."

"Okay." The once-over he gave her in the rearview mirror told her he wasn't quite convinced.

Two blocks later, she was talking to herself again. "I'm leaving it to fate."

"Fate, miss?"

"Yes." She nodded. "If he's not in, I'll simply have you take me to my apartment, where I'll pass the evening. Alone. With my cat."

"Very good."

Easy for the cabby to say. He didn't know her cat. *Please, God! Let Simon be home.*

Mrs. Benson answered the door. The older woman was holding her purse, clearly ready to call it a day. Even so, her smile remained in place at Chloe's unexpected intrusion. And, if she noticed Chloe's unnatural color, she didn't let it show.

"Good evening, Miss McDaniels. Mr. Ford didn't tell me you would be dropping by."

"I...I didn't know myself. I was just...in the neighborhood and thought I'd take a chance." She waved the bouquet. "Is he in?"

"He just arrived a few minutes ago."

"Fate," Chloe whispered.

"Excuse me?"

"Nothing."

"Come in and make yourself at home. Can I get you a cocktail?"

She probably shouldn't. Her stomach had only just settled. "I would love one." She smiled. "And a breath mint if you have one."

Simon paced the expanse of his bedroom. According to Mrs. Benson, Chloe was seated on his couch enjoying a drink. He shouldn't be nervous. After all, he'd called her at her workplace earlier and had asked her to dinner with the very hope of seeing her tonight. He'd wanted to be sure that he hadn't done anything to permanently damage a friendship that he cherished beyond all others. He'd felt disappointed when she'd declined his invitation. Nervous and a little sick at heart. But he'd also been relieved. As much as he needed to talk to her, he wasn't ready to face her.

The kiss he'd already apologized for was front and center on his mind. He wanted to do it again. More thoroughly. He felt like a starving man who'd been given a glimpse of a grand buffet. One brief taste of her was hardly enough.

He'd never met another woman who could inspire, excite or, for that matter, exasperate him more. She was the standard by which he measured other women, and even before college he'd figured out no one else would ever come close. He'd given up trying to find someone like her. He'd settled for women who, in many ways, were her polar opposite. In a weird way, he'd hoped they would prove to be the antidote to whatever spell she'd cast over him.

A decade later, he knew. It was no spell. His feelings

for her were the real thing. Chloe meant everything to him. Which was why he felt so nervous now. What would he do if he lost her?

In the living room, one look at her face and he forgot all about his problems. She looked…shell-shocked.

"My God, Chloe. Is everything all right?"

"Do you mean beyond the fact that I'm orange, date-less for our upcoming reunion and now unemployed?" She sipped her drink. The hand holding the glass tumbler wasn't quite steady.

"Unemployed?"

"Yes."

Outrage had Simon's hands curling into fists at his sides. "That son of… He fired you?"

She sipped her drink again and was shaking her head even before she swallowed. "No, no, no. See, if I'd been fired, I would be able to file for unemployment benefits." Hysterical laughter followed. "Gee, Frannie didn't even think to rub *that* in my face."

Simon settled onto the cushion next to her. He needed a road map to follow this conversation. "When did you speak to Frannie?"

"Before I came here. I threw up in the box of my personal effects afterward." She made a face, but then shrugged philosophically. "It didn't really matter. It was no great loss. I mean, for the most part it was just a nameplate, business cards and some outdated floppy discs. Who uses floppies anymore?"

"Exactly."

"And that plant, it was a goner anyway."

He wasn't going to ask.

"The flowers you sent me were spared. They're lovely, by the way. And so was the bouquet you sent to my apartment last night. Thank you."

He acknowledged her gratitude with a nod. "So, you quit your job?"

"I did." She smiled in an overly bright fashion before taking another liberal swig of her drink, which was nearly gone by this point. "No more Miss Nice Gal. I told Mr. Thompson that I was through being taken for granted. Only one of his full-time people could work tonight, despite the importance of the account. But good old Chloe...." She wagged the glass in front of Simon's nose. Ice cubes clinked together. "It was just like you said. He was taking advantage of me."

Of all the days to listen to him, Chloe *would* pick today. Well, he'd be supportive. She needed him. That's why she was here. She was looking for a shoulder to lean on. He scooted over on the couch and put his arm around her, not as the man who wanted to make love with her, but as the man who loved her. Who would *always* love her. And he offered her that very shoulder.

"You're going to be fine."

"Of course I am." Her head came to rest in the crook of his neck.

"Your talents are in demand."

"Yep. High demand. Regardless of the lousy economy." She nodded vigorously. Her hair tickled his nose and smelled phenomenal.

"Regardless," he agreed, inhaling deeply a second time.

"You believe in me." She angled her head and smiled at him.

"Always."

Chloe moistened her lips and her gaze strayed to his mouth. He recognized interest when he saw it. Panic built right along with desire. All it would take was a simple pivoting of their positions and she would be beneath him on the couch. Then he could lose himself in her soft curves as he had so many times in his fantasies.

He straightened, forcing her to, as well.

"D-do you want to work on your resume?" he asked.

"Not right now."

"That's right. You're still in the wallowing stage."

He knew the stages Chloe went through after life handed her a lemon as well as he knew the back of his hand. Wallowing came first and involved food and three-hanky movies. She'd be hitting him up for ice cream any minute and wanting to know what was playing on cable.

"I was wallowing. That's one of the reasons I came here." Her expression remained sober. "But I just realized it wasn't the only reason."

"No?"

"I can count on you."

He relaxed a little. "Always."

"Simon, do you…do you think I'm adorable?"

It was an odd question, but he didn't think twice before answering. "Of course I do."

"But I'm not your type, am I?"

"Um…" Again, a map would have come in handy to follow the direction of the conversation.

That's when Chloe took him over the cliff. "Simon, why did you kiss me?"

"I shouldn't have."

She finished off her drink, setting the tumbler aside afterward. He waited for her to rise, expected her to leave, and prayed that she would do so without crying.

Her eyes weren't the least bit moist when she demanded, "Why? Aren't you interested in me?"

"We're friends, Chloe." He stood.

"That's not an answer." She shot to her feet, as well.

"What's gotten into you?" He forced out a laugh.

She wasn't put off. She poked his chest with her index finger. Another time, he would admire her tenacity and spirit. "Don't you dare. If anyone around here is entitled to ask that question, it's me. You've been sending me all sorts of mixed signals these past several weeks."

She had him there. "Okay, okay." He sucked in a breath, exhaled. "I find you...attractive." What a pathetic understatement that was.

"Is that supposed to be some sort of revelation?" He blanched when she added, "I figured that out for myself when we danced at your father's wedding."

He spat out an oath and scrubbed a hand over his face, but it wasn't only embarrassment he felt. At the moment, he was every bit as hard and tempted as he'd been that night.

Chloe nearly let the matter drop. His expression told her she was playing with fire. And, God help her, she'd never been more turned on in her life. Her hormones were humming in a way she'd never experienced even during foreplay.

A moment ago, Simon had asked what had gotten into her. She wasn't sure. She only knew she was sick of the status quo. She was taking charge of her life. She wanted to be in control of her destiny. It was what had prompted her to quit her job earlier. And what drove her now.

She pushed aside the recollection of barfing not long after drawing a line in the sand with Mr. Thompson.

"I have another question for you, Simon."

Here it was. The point of no return. Ask this question and nothing would ever be the same between them, assuming he answered honestly. And even if he lied, their relationship would shift.

"Do you think you'll ever kiss me again the way you did in your office?"

His brows tugged together, but before he could say anything, Chloe forged ahead. This was like her workouts. No pain, no gain. "I'm asking, because I liked it. A lot. And I've been thinking about it. A lot. I've been thinking about *you* a lot, for that matter. Even before that kiss, I was…curious."

"Curious about what?"

She took the fact that his voice cracked as a good sign.

"You. I've always admired your hands. I've wondered what they would feel like. On me. And I'm not talking about a mere foot massage, however delicious I found the one you gave me after the party."

"Chloe—"

"Getting back to that kiss. Will you?"

The gauntlet had been tossed down. Would he pick it up?

"No."

Her lungs deflated to the point she wasn't sure she would be capable of sucking in breath again. Since a graceful exit was out of the question, she was determined to at least wait till she made it to the elevator before she fell apart completely. Simon grabbed her arm before she could brush past him.

"I'm going to kiss you like this."

What she'd experienced that day in his office was tepid in comparison. His mouth was hot and demanding. The hands she'd complimented earlier were fisted in her hair. He tilted her head to one side and began to kiss and nip his way down her neck.

"I love your skin," he murmured.

"I love your mouth."

The mouth in question came back to hers. His hands were no longer in her hair, but at the front of her blouse, working the buttons free. She decided to return the favor, eager to revel in that first touch of skin to skin.

His hands fumbled at the back of her bra.

"The clasp is in the front," she whispered.

Need like she'd never known built as he brought his hands around and his fingers traced the V of her cleavage. The underwire had been a good call today. And fate had been looking out for her when she'd gone with lace panties, even though they had a tendency to ride up. It was then she realized, Simon had stopped caressing her.

"We can't do this, Chloe. As much as I want to, we can't."

A bucket of ice water wouldn't have been as effective. He'd better have a good reason for stopping, like they were related by blood. What he said floored her. Not so much the words as his doomed expression.

"I love you, Chloe." He plucked her blouse off the floor and put it around her shoulders.

She swallowed. "Just to clarify, when you say you love me, are you talking love with a capital *L* or love with a small *l?*"

"Capital *L.*"

Go figure. The only man who'd ever said that to her and he was using the words to talk her *out* of sleeping with him. She didn't know whether to laugh or cry. She did neither.

She got mad.

"Why haven't you said something?"

"I don't want things between us to change."

"They already have! They've been changing." She blinked, shook her head. "You've lied to me, Simon. I can't believe you, of all people, lied to me."

"I haven't lied."

"Well, you haven't been honest." She pushed her arms into the sleeves of her blouse and wrapped it over her chest. "I don't understand. You're interested in me and you date…everybody but me."

"You haven't exactly lived like a nun."

"No. And you've always been there for the breakups. A perfect friend. But you were glad, weren't you?"

"I won't pretend I was sorry. None of them was good enough for you."

"Who is good enough for me, Simon? Hmm?"

He snagged his own shirt off the floor and said nothing as he shoved his arms into it.

"Or maybe I'm getting ahead of myself. Maybe you don't think I'm good enough for you," she pressed.

He flung the shirt aside, grabbed her by the arms and gave her a little shake. Relief and a wave of love flooded through her at his outraged expression.

"Don't say that! Don't even think it! That's not the reason I've kept my feelings to myself."

"Then what is?"

"I need you in my life."

"I'm not going anywhere."

His hands dropped away. "Clarissa said that, too. She promised. But being around my father after their divorce was just too painful because she still loved him. As much as love can bind people together, it can drive them apart, too. If we become lovers, we won't be able to go back to being just friends. That's why I've always been so careful with you, Chloe."

"Oh, Simon."

She reached for him, but he backed away, shaking his head. His throat worked spasmodically.

"None of the women I've ever dated has mattered to me. But you... I can't risk losing you. I won't."

She swallowed. No man had ever said anything half as romantic. Or half as heartbreaking.

She buttoned her blouse and gathered up her things. "You're risking that now."

Then she walked out the door.

CHAPTER THIRTEEN

Cutest Couple

CHLOE'S COMPLEXION WAS nearly back to normal by the day of the reunion. Funny, but she didn't care. The reunion was no longer such a big deal.

Oh, she was still attending. She needed to exorcise some demons and come to terms with her past. She'd never truly move on otherwise. Simon's struggle with his past made that crystal clear. He was willing to deny himself a romantic relationship with Chloe as a result of the hurt he'd felt as a child.

So, yes, she was attending, but she was going as herself. She canceled the appointment to have her hair professionally straightened, and she'd returned the third little black dress, since it still had the tags on it. Instead of the color of mourning, she decided to wear the copper-hued number she'd worn to Simon's cocktail party.

Simon. She had no doubt the man loved her. He'd arranged a party at his apartment so she could try to get Trevor's attention. It must have killed him.

Chloe knew she wanted to kill him.

But mostly, she just wanted him back. Even if friendship was all he could ever offer her.

She hadn't told him that, though. In fact, they hadn't spoken since that evening in his apartment. He hadn't called her and she couldn't bring herself to call him. How could she? The ball was in his court.

She wanted to burn with embarrassment when she thought of what had transpired between them, mostly at her urging. She burned, all right. But it had little to do with embarrassment.

And so she dressed for the reunion not with a sense of anticipation or triumph, despite her newly toned figure, but eager to have the evening behind her.

The old gym was nearly unrecognizable when Chloe arrived, as were many of her former classmates. She glanced around the sea of faces, hoping to spy a familiar one. Wouldn't it just figure her gaze landed on Tamara, Faith and Natasha?

Oh, they'd changed a little. They'd somehow managed to become more beautiful. And each was as thin and shapely as they'd been in their cheerleading days. The men they were with were gorgeous, even by Trevor standards. No doubt they all had successful careers going while Chloe remained unemployed.

Her newfound confidence began to wilt. She was sixteen again, frizzy-haired, freckled and bespectacled, standing in the middle of Tillman High's cafeteria with a tray of food and nowhere to sit. The exit beckoned, but she squared her shoulders.

She felt a hand at the small of her back then and glanced to the side to find Simon there. The man she loved. Just as importantly, the friend she needed.

She hadn't allowed herself to cry since the night she'd left his apartment. Her eyes filled now.

"I didn't think—"

"That I would come?"

"After what happened, what I said."

"You spoke your mind."

"I didn't mean it."

"No?"

"You aren't risking anything. I don't want things between us to change, either, if it means not having you in my life at all. I've been miserable these past couple of weeks. We've always been friends. Let's keep it that way."

"So, you want things to go back to the way they were between us before?"

"Yes. No… It depends on what you want."

"I vote for before." But he was grinning. "As in before I got stupid and made you put your shirt back on."

She blinked. Could she have heard him right? The pull low in her belly suggested yes, but she asked, "Can you repeat that?"

"How about I repeat this—I love you, Chloe. I always have. I always will."

The tears broke free, no doubt taking some of her mascara with them. "Just to clarify, you're not talking as a friend? Right?"

"How about if I kiss you and leave it to you to decide?"

He left no room for doubt as to his interest or intentions for later that evening. In fact, she didn't want to wait.

"I think we should leave."

Simon grinned. "So soon?"

"I came. I saw. I conquered."

She waved at Natasha, Faith and Tamara, who now were staring at them slack-jawed, apparently having witnessed the kiss. The good-looking men they were with had nothing on Simon. And the unholy trinity had nothing on Chloe. Simon had said so all along. Her champion and protector and dearest friend. The man she wanted to spend the rest of her life with...he'd been right there all along.

"How ironic."

"What?" Simon asked.

"It took until our ten-year reunion for me to figure out that you were my high school sweetheart."

He kissed her quick and hard. Her heart bucked and that was before he said, "As long as it doesn't take you until our twentieth to figure out a date for our wedding."

Harlequin® *Romance*

Coming Next Month

Available September 13, 2011

#4261 THE LONESOME RANCHER
The Quilt Shop in Kerry Springs
Patricia Thayer

#4262 ROYAL WEDDING BELLS
Raye Morgan and Nina Harrington

#4263 THE PRINCESS TEST
Once Upon a Kiss...
Shirley Jump

#4264 RESCUED BY THE BROODING TYCOON
The Falcon Dynasty
Lucy Gordon

#4265 SWEPT OFF HER STILETTOS
The Fun Factor
Fiona Harper

#4266 THE HEART OF A HERO
Barbara Wallace

You can find more information on upcoming
Harlequin® titles, free excerpts and more at
www.HarlequinInsideRomance.com.

HRCNM0811

REQUEST YOUR FREE BOOKS!
2 FREE NOVELS PLUS 2 FREE GIFTS!

Harlequin® Romance

From the Heart, For the Heart

YES! Please send me 2 FREE Harlequin® Romance novels and my 2 FREE gifts (gifts are worth about $10). After receiving them, if I don't wish to receive any more books, I can return the shipping statement marked "cancel". If I don't cancel, I will receive 6 brand-new novels every month and be billed just $4.09 per book in the U.S. or $4.49 per book in Canada. That's a savings of at least 14% off the cover price! It's quite a bargain! Shipping and handling is just 50¢ per book in the U.S. and 75¢ per book in Canada.* I understand that accepting the 2 free books and gifts places me under no obligation to buy anything. I can always return a shipment and cancel at any time. Even if I never buy another book, the two free books and gifts are mine to keep forever.

116/316 HDN FESE

Name	(PLEASE PRINT)	

Address		Apt. #

City	State/Prov.	Zip/Postal Code

Signature (if under 18, a parent or guardian must sign)

Mail to the **Reader Service:**
IN U.S.A.: P.O. Box 1867, Buffalo, NY 14240-1867
IN CANADA: P.O. Box 609, Fort Erie, Ontario L2A 5X3

Not valid for current subscribers to Harlequin Romance books.

**Are you a subscriber to Harlequin Romance books
and want to receive the larger-print edition?
Call 1-800-873-8635 or visit www.ReaderService.com.**

* Terms and prices subject to change without notice. Prices do not include applicable taxes. Sales tax applicable in N.Y. Canadian residents will be charged applicable taxes. Offer not valid in Quebec. This offer is limited to one order per household. All orders subject to credit approval. Credit or debit balances in a customer's account(s) may be offset by any other outstanding balance owed by or to the customer. Please allow 4 to 6 weeks for delivery. Offer available while quantities last.

Your Privacy—The Reader Service is committed to protecting your privacy. Our Privacy Policy is available online at www.ReaderService.com or upon request from the Reader Service.

We make a portion of our mailing list available to reputable third parties that offer products we believe may interest you. If you prefer that we not exchange your name with third parties, or if you wish to clarify or modify your communication preferences, please visit us at www.ReaderService.com/consumerschoice or write to us at Reader Service Preference Service, P.O. Box 9062, Buffalo, NY 14269. Include your complete name and address.

HRI1B

New York Times *and* USA TODAY *bestselling author*
Maya Banks presents a brand-new miniseries

PREGNANCY & PASSION

When four irresistible tycoons face
the consequences of temptation.

Book 1—ENTICED BY HIS FORGOTTEN LOVER

Available September 2011 from Harlequin® Desire®!

Rafael de Luca had been in bad situations before. A crowded ballroom could never make him sweat.

These people would never know that he had no memory of any of them.

He surveyed the party with grim tolerance, searching for the source of his unease.

At first his gaze flickered past her, but he yanked his attention back to a woman across the room. Her stare bored holes through him. Unflinching and steady, even when his eyes locked with hers.

Petite, even in heels, she had a creamy olive complexion. A wealth of inky-black curls cascaded over her shoulders and her eyes were equally dark.

She looked at him as if she'd already judged him and found him lacking. He'd never seen her before in his life. Or had he?

He cursed the gaping hole in his memory. He'd been diagnosed with selective amnesia after his accident four months ago. Which seemed like complete and utter bull. No one got amnesia except hysterical women in bad soap operas.

With a smile, he disengaged himself from the group

around him and made his way to the mystery woman.

She wasn't coy. She stared straight at him as he approached, her chin thrust upward in defiance.

"Excuse me, but have we met?" he asked in his smoothest voice.

His gaze moved over the generous swell of her breasts pushed up by the empire waist of her black cocktail dress.

When he glanced back up at her face, he saw fury in her eyes.

"Have we *met?*" Her voice was barely a whisper, but he felt each word like the crack of a whip.

Before he could process her response, she nailed him with a right hook. He stumbled back, holding his nose.

One of his guards stepped between Rafe and the woman, accidentally sending her to one knee. Her hand flew to the folds of her dress.

It was then, as she cupped her belly, that the realization hit him. She was pregnant.

Her eyes flashing, she turned and ran down the marble hallway.

Rafael ran after her. He burst from the hotel lobby, and saw two shoes sparkling in the moonlight, twinkling at him.

He blew out his breath in frustration and then shoved the pair of sparkly, ultrafeminine heels at his head of security.

"Find the woman who wore these shoes."

Will Rafael find his mystery woman?
Find out in Maya Banks's passionate new novel
ENTICED BY HIS FORGOTTEN LOVER
Available September 2011 from Harlequin® Desire®!